Ellen Richardson resides outside of Houston, Texas. She has always been an avid reader of mystery stories. A passion for completing complicated puzzles motivated her to begin writing mysteries. She enjoys traveling, especially cruises to warm places with family members.

I would like to dedicate this book to my family and friends
who have always supported my writing.

Ellen Richardson

MURDER AND THE TALK SHOW DIVA

AUSTIN MACAULEY PUBLISHERS™

LONDON · CAMBRIDGE · NEW YORK · SHARJAH

Ordering Information
Quantity sales: Special discounts are available on quantity purchases by corporations, associations, and others. For details, contact the publisher at the address below.

Publisher's Cataloging-in-Publication data
Richardson, Ellen
Murder and the Talk Show Diva

ISBN 9781647504540 (Paperback)
ISBN 9781647504557 (ePub e-book)

Library of Congress Control Number: 2020917919

www.austinmacauley.com/us

First Published (2020)
Austin Macauley Publishers LLC
40 Wall Street, 28th Floor
New York, NY 10005
USA

mail-usa@austinmacauley.com
+1 (646) 5125767

I would like to thank my sister, JoAnn Blake, who unselfishly gave her time and effort in helping me complete this book. Her comments, critiques, and willingness to be my sounding board were invaluable.

Chapter One

Cassandra Clark turned her desk chair around and glared across the desk at her personal assistant, Delilah Morgan. "I can't believe it, Delilah. Lately, when I've given you a simple assignment you never seem to get it right. What's wrong with you?"

Delilah looked up from her notes and silently thought, *Cassandra Clark, known in Houston as 'CC', KLS radio talk show host and infamous newspaper gossip columnist, again blaming me for a mistake she herself had made.* She longed to scream back at her, "What's wrong with you!"

"You know how important tonight's party is to me and you picked up the wrong dress, I wouldn't be caught dead in that red rag you just had delivered." CC looked over in disgust at the dress hanging on the back of her office door.

Delilah stood up, "But CC, that's the dress you told me to order, I wrote it down. Style number…" Before she could finish, Norma the radio station receptionist stuck her head in the door then walked into the office.

Swinging her intricately braided hairdo and huge gold earrings Norma walked over to CC's desk and laid two pink messages on her desk. "Crisis averted. Your housekeeper just called; your new dress has just been delivered."

Grabbing Delilah's arm, Norma quickly ushered Delilah out of CC's office. Turning around Norma announced to CC, "Your hairstylist and makeup artist also called they will both be at your house at 5:30. Better get a move on."

Delilah stood outside CC's door again examining her notes. "Norma, I know I didn't make a mistake with the dress."

"You didn't make a mistake, honey, her stylist confirmed CC ordered the red dress. CC will realize she's the one who made the mistake when she opens the shoe box with the shoes she personally ordered are bright red; I would pay to see the look on her face."

Norma stood in the opening of Delilah's small cubicle and looked down at Delilah's sad face.

"I don't know what's gotten into CC. When I first started working for her, years ago, she was a mentor; sometimes almost like a mother." Delilah sighed with a shrug of her shoulders.

"I can tell by the smirk on your face, Norma, you don't believe me. Sure, she sends me on a million silly errands, works me into the wee hours of the morning with little or no real appreciation, but if I made a mistake it wasn't the end of the world. Nowadays when I make a mistake, I just sit back and wait for the fallout."

"You forget, Delilah, CC hired me long before you came on board. In the years CC and I worked together, we have only had one confrontation. In that confrontation, she quickly learned I was not going to put up with her attitude. She learned to walk just a little softly around me. She also learned that I was extremely loyal to her. That's why she's put up with me and MY attitude over the years."

Norma took the notebook Delilah was clutching in her hand and laid it on her desk. "Get your things together and go home. CC will be leaving soon and KLS' illustrious station manager, Jerry Wainwright left hours ago to get ready for the party."

"Norma, what is so important about this party?"

Norma leaned in the cubicle and whispered, "It's rumored that John McIntyre who's giving the party, is in deep financial trouble. He has invited some of the richest people in town to the party. He's trying to scare up money for his latest project."

"What does that have to do with CC?"

"CC smells blood in the water. She's looking for dirt either to put in her column or to spread gossip on her radio show. She seldom mentions any one's real name in her column or on the radio, but tomorrow people will be looking over their shoulder wondering who she's talking about."

"Why is Jerry going to the party?"

"Both Jerry and John are both trolling the party for the same dollars. Jerry for the radio station: John for any dollars he can find."

"Go home, Delilah, and enjoy your weekend. As for me, it's margaritas at my favorite restaurant with friends. As far as I'm concerned, KLS will not be mentioned or worried about until Monday morning." Norma turned quickly and left the cubicle.

Delilah started straightening her desk. Turning off her desk light, she grabbed her purse and headed for the parking lot.

Norma was standing outside the station fanning with a newspaper. When Delilah stepped outside, Norma looked Delilah up and down. "Why don't you join our group for Happy Hour?; A little time with the girls tonight might be just what is needed."

"Where are you all meeting," Delilah asked hesitantly.

"We're meeting at Snookies of course. Snookies is only a short drive from your house. It may look like a hole in the wall but it has great tapas and half-price drinks during happy hour." Norma reached in her purse and pulled out a coupon. She waved the coupon in front of Delilah's face.

"This baby will get the two of us half-price tapas. What do you say?"

"Maybe I'll join you later. Right now, I'm looking forward to taking off these shoes and cooling off when I get home."

Seeing the frown on Norma's face, Delilah added "How long will you be there?"

"Who knows," Norma said laughing, "Happy hour ends at 7:00 PM but we have been known to linger longer. Come on down." Norma gave her a wave and walked to her car.

****

After driving through congested rush hour traffic, Delilah arrived at her front door. She entered her house and realized right away she couldn't stay there. The thermostat hovered near 85 degrees. She tried a light switch: nothing happened. A call to the electric company confirmed a power outage for the neighborhood was in the process of being repaired; the estimated time of completion was 7:00 PM.

Delilah laughed. *This is definitely a sign that I need to join Norma for Happy Hour.*

Delilah went into the bathroom and looked at herself in the mirror. The face that stared back was showing signs of the heat. She removed her glasses and unbraided the long thick braid that hung halfway down her back, washed her face, and put on lipstick. *Not great but better* Delilah didn't want to think about getting back in traffic with her car. She picked up her phone and called Uber to order a ride.

Chapter Two

Four Hours Later

CC watched as a buxom redhead walked toward her from across the room. The unbelievable behemoth was dressed in a hideous orange dress two sizes too small. *This unbelievable creature was Joyce and John's surprise guest? What a joke.* Joyce had confided to CC earlier that this horrible creature wrote novels that exposed the well-kept secrets of the rich and famous. "You two have a lot in common," Joyce had said and laughed over the phone. *A lot in common* CC thought to herself; *I have nothing in common with this country bumpkin.* Pasting a smile on her face CC watched the feather-bedecked creature bearing down on her. She tried not to grimace when the woman smiled and pumped her hand in a bone-crushing handshake.

"Clarisse Coburn. My friends call me CC too." She giggled.

"We have a lot in common; the same initials and a nose for the news. It is so nice to finally meet the famous Cassandra Clark; I hear you're a household word in this town." CC winced when Clarisse slapped her on the back.

I'm bigger than Houston, CC thought, withdrawing her crushed fingers from Clarisse's iron grip. For the next 30 minutes, while desperately scanning the crowd for her husband, Robert Clarke, CC listened to Clarisse's incessant chatter. Her only hope was that she was nodding and smiling at Clarisse in the right places. *You owe me big time for this Joyce. This better be a phenomenal party or I'll crucify you and your husband in my column* CC thought silently. CC watched helplessly as Clarisse, once again, scrolled through her phone for more pictures of her grandchildren.

Snagging a glass of Champagne from a passing waiter, CC drank the entire contents without missing a beat. She tried desperately to distance herself from Clarisse but the woman clung to her like a second skin. Pushing her way through the crowd, CC tried to lose Clarisse but the woman was hot on her trail. If she turned to the right, Clarisse was standing to her right. If she turned to her left, Clarisse was standing on her left. *What did she want? Why can't she leave me alone?* CC was on her fourth glass of Champagne when she finally spotted Robert, across the room and signaled him to join her.

When Robert saw her expression, he immediately excused himself from the boisterous group of oilmen he had been joking with and made his way across the room toward her. In her present drunken state, she didn't know whether she admired Robert more for his graceful muscular body or his boyishly candid eyes. No, she decided instantly, she admired him most for his always immediate response to the 'I need your help' expression on her face. He knew that look so very well and as usual, responded quickly.

CC smiled as Robert approached. *Robert Clark, my own personal creation, she thought to herself.* When he first arrived in Houston, he had been as rough and coarse as Ms. Clarissa Coburn. The only difference between the two was he came to town with a pile of cash and no real idea what to do with it. She had carefully orchestrated Robert's success, groomed him in every area she thought was important, and made sure all the right doors were opened for him; he had successfully done the rest on his own. He had made it big in the oil business. He had been transformed from oilfield roustabout to oil multi-millionaire. Robert had successfully branched out from the oil business and made a fortune. CC felt she was directly responsible for his success whether he gave her credit or not.

"Robert, darling, I'd like you to meet Clarisse Coburn. Clarisse, this is my husband Robert Clark." CC smiled and possessively put her arm around Robert's waist.

Clarisse's mouth dropped open in disbelief. "Robert?" Clarisse muttered.

"Robert Clark," she repeated.

"Bobby Joe Clark is that you?" Clarisse again dug into her small bag this time pulling out a pair of rhinestone eyeglasses. She quickly put them on and stared up at Robert.

"Hot damn it is you. You probably don't remember me: I was a year behind you in Gaylord High School. Hell, you probably don't remember me at all; back then I was a Jenkins, Clarisse Jenkins."

CC quickly looked around the room. To her besotted mind, it seemed as if everyone in the room was looking and listening to them. Clarisse's vulgar laugh sounded extremely loud, or was it the four glasses of champagne that was making her ears ring?

"Look at you all dressed up and citified." Clarisse patted the front of Robert's suit.

"Imagine you married one of my new best friends – Cassandra Clark. My, you've come a long way from Gaylord, Texas, but again, so have I."

Always the gentleman, Robert flashed her smile and extended his hand. "It's not often you run across someone from Gaylord, Texas. Welcome to Houston, Ms. Coburn."

He thought for a moment. "Yes, I do remember the Jenkins brothers – Hank and Dave; we all worked together in the oilfields. The Jenkins family was always very kind to me."

Clarisse beamed. "We were all considered oilfield trash back then but look at us now." She elbowed Robert in the ribs. Robert didn't seem the least bit embarrassed.

Yes, well you are still oilfield trash, CC thought grimly draining another glass of Champagne. *You really think you've struck it rich, don't you? Bobby Joe Clark? Bobby Joe Clark died years ago and I brought him back as Robert Clark. He's my dream, my creation, my success.* She continued to silently fume. *Enjoy your fifteen minutes of fame, Clarisse Coburn. I'll mention you and this pathetic party in my column, then I've fulfilled my obligation to Joyce and John McIntyre; no more favors.* CC slammed her empty Champagne glass down on the table and picked up another glass from a passing waiter.

"I can't believe you're married to Cassandra Clark. What a surprise." She leaned over and spoke to CC in a voice that was guaranteed to wake the dead.

"This man here married the daughter of one of the richest oilmen in west Texas, swindled her father out of a fortune then disappeared. Whatever happened to your first wife, Virginia Miller, and your baby girl? You left town first, then Virginia and the baby. We all thought you two must have hooked up somewhere later; neither one of you ever came back to Gaylord. What happened?"

Before he could answer she slowly shook her head. "When Virginia's father realized he had lost his business, all his money; his wife, daughter, and granddaughter, it's no wonder he nearly drank himself to death. Hot damn, Bobby Joe, your story could possibly be my next book; I can smell a best seller."

CC felt her hand tighten around her champagne glass. Grabbing Robert's arm, she gasped, "I fear my migraine has come back. Let's say good night to our host and go home." Clarisse's loud revelation and CC's hurried departure drew the attention of many people standing nearby. Every eye in the room seemed to be on them as CC guided Robert through the crowd.

Chapter Three

The valet extended car keys to Robert, which CC immediately snatched out of his hands. She got into the driver's seat, fastened her seat belt, and glared out the window as Robert walked to the passenger side and got into the car. He barely fastened his seat belt before she stomped on the accelerator and tore down the street. Robert didn't say a word when she drove past their street, nor did he comment when she accelerated onto the freeway.

Wiping the tears from her cheeks with the back of her hand, she glanced at her husband who sat slouched in the seat next to her. If her speed or erratic driving bothered him, he gave no indication. He lit a cigar, took a deep breath, then blew perfect rings of cigar smoke into the air; slowly and silently drawing a smoky curtain between them.

"How could you do this to me?" she shouted, pounding the steering wheel with her fist.

Robert casually looked over at her drawn face. "Do what?" he said.

"Let the public know where I really came from. I'm not ashamed of my past, but you are. I'm sorry you had to find out about my past that way, CC. I should have told you years ago. But…" He searched for the right word.

"Haven't you ever had something in your past you'd like to forget or at least put it behind you? Trust me – what happened tonight will blow over," Robert said quietly.

"Blow over," she shouted taking one hand off the steering wheel as she gestured wildly with her hand. "I stand there, like a complete idiot, in a crowd with some of our closest friends, as I'm casually informed that not only am I the second Mrs. Robert Clark but that you also have another daughter. A wife and daughter you've conveniently failed to mention for over thirty years. Oh, let's not leave out that you are a thief, married the old man's daughter, stole all his money, and ran off and left your wife and baby and you have the nerve to tell me 'It will blow over.'"

"If anyone overheard the conversation CC, they probably thought you already knew I had been married before. What are you worried about? My first marriage ended years before I met you…"

He paused, again trying to find the right words. "As for the child, I've only seen my daughter – once."

He nervously blew another cloud of smoke into the air. "It's strange but for the past few years, I've seriously wondered what happened to my daughter. Has she ever tried to find me? Should I try to find her? Would she still want me in her life after all these years? Those questions have been bothering me a lot lately."

CC completely ignored the twinge of sadness in his voice. "Spare me the dramatics," she spat.

"Did you even bother to divorce her before you married me?" CC screamed.

When he didn't reply to her question, she knew the answer. "What do you think this is going to do to my career, my social standing? What about our children?"

Robert gave an audible sign. "As usual your career is your first priority. I wish you could hear yourself. Have you ever noticed that whenever you list the things that are important in your life, my name is never mentioned?"

"I've already told you that KLS Radio has cut my talk show down to 30 minutes and the Chronicle is canceling my weekly column. This whole town has been waiting for years to bring me down."

"YOU," she said stabbing her finger at him.

"You may have just provided the ammunition they need to bring me down and I'm powerless to stop it."

"Is that what this is all about, CC, power? There was a time when the mere mention of a name in your column or on the radio, could make or break anyone in this town. You used that power with total disregard for the harm you might cause; it was all for the ratings. There are probably quite a few people in this town that would like to bring you down but I'm not one of them."

Robert unbuckled his seat belt and leaned forward to put out his cigar. "There's another decision I've made a while ago, I wrote a new will. The bulk of my fortune will go to you in the new will; the remainder will be split equally between my THREE children."

She started at him in disbelief. "You mean to say you plan to leave some of your money to some nameless, faceless child? I won't allow it."

"You have no choice. I've made up my mind. Think about it CC, both of our children have never left home.

They've done absolutely nothing with their lives. Oh, let's not forgot their social life. They've managed to keep that afloat." He started ticking off items on his fingers.

"We financed their trip to New York for Shelby's brilliant modeling career and Preston's writing of the great American novel. Two months later, they're back in Houston never coming clean about what happened in New York and their sudden return to the nest."

CC seemed completely oblivious to Robert. "Oh, don't worry, CC after I'm gone they'll run through their money very quickly and be under your thumb in a matter of months. After all these years I'm going to be the new sheriff in town." He laughed.

"Things are going to change in the Clark household."

"How can you do this to me, Robert? My whole life is falling apart. The gossip and innuendoes alone will slowly kill me off."

"You've dealt in gossip and innuendoes your entire life; that's what your newspaper column and radio shows are all about. You're the queen of gossip – sugar coated with all your good, sound, advice. Now the tables are turned on you. Let's see if all your River Oaks buddies stand behind you now. Lord only knows you've knifed then in the back more than once."

"My friends and public adore me." CC spat at him.

"Your friends have tolerated you because they were always afraid of what you would do to their lives with your vicious gossiping. Anything you could dig up on them was fair game; you thrived on it. Now you feel your power base slipping and suddenly you're afraid. Finally, there's some juicy gossip on Cassandra Clark." CC started to cry.

CC's tears didn't stop Robert's angry tirade. He held his hand up as if he was holding a microphone and said in a scathing voice. "Listen, folks, Cassandra Clark has always been so kind and thoughtful to all of us: let's not gossip about her, it's just not fair. Now, will all of Cassandra's *real friends* please stand up? What, no one is standing up." His booming laughter filled the car.

"You monster," CC screamed as she swerved to miss a truck stalled in her lane. She tried to slow down but the powerful car roared down the freeway as if it had a mind of its own. In a split second the Jaguar hit the truck, spun across the freeway, bounced against the guardrail, and flipped over the embankment. The hazy-gray smoke from the crusted black car greeted the morning commuters as they attempted to drive through the early morning traffic.

Chapter Four

Delilah Morgan woke to the shrill ringing of her cell phone. Rolling over, she glanced at the clock, she could not believe someone was calling her this early in the morning. Shaking her head to relieve the effects of too many Margaritas, Delilah reached for the annoying instrument. *This better be good or someone is in big trouble.*

"Delilah, this is Jerry Wainwright. I want you to come to the Medical Center right now. CC and Robert have been in an automobile accident and CC is in the emergency room."

Jerry was the station manager for KLS radio where Delilah worked as a Personal Assistant to Cassandra Clark. Delilah's first thought was that maybe one of the targets of CC's vicious gossip might have finally decided to strike back.

Jerry was practically screaming into the phone, "She's in surgery at Houston Methodist Hospital in the Medical Center. GET DOWN HERE NOW," he shouted.

"I'm on my way, Delilah shouted back, aren't you needed at the station to handle the press?"

"I've already called Norma, she'll take care of everything today; now get down here right away."

****

When Delilah ran into the waiting room near the ICU, she spotted Jerry on the phone near a large floor to ceiling window. His face was an unnatural shade of red. He turned and glared at Delilah. "It took you long enough to get here."

"What's going on? Is CC going to be alright?" Delilah asked as she approached Jerry.

"No, she is not alright. She ran that car of hers into a stalled truck and it rolled down an embankment. Fortunately, she survived but Robert didn't. The police have determined that the car was traveling at a very high rate of speed and CC was intoxicated. Based on what happened earlier in the evening at the McIntyre's party, I can't blame her. She was probably very upset and angry and not really paying attention."

Delilah pulled Jerry over to a row of empty seats and they sat down. "What happened at the party?"

Jerry quickly told her the story.

"In a nutshell that's what happened at the party; it must have thrown CC into a rage." Jerry leaned back in his chair and closed his eyes.

"What a mess."

Delilah couldn't believe what she was hearing. Before she could ask any questions, a tall gray-haired doctor in blue scrubs entered the room. "I understand that the two of you here for Mrs. Clark? We've had no luck trying to reach her children."

"This is Jerry Wainwright her boss at KLS Radio. I'm Delilah Morgan her Personal Assistant; Will she be alright?"

"She came through surgery and is being moved to a room in the intensive care unit. She survived but has a long recovery period ahead of her. It's unclear now how much residual damage there will be from the accident; we will just have to wait and see. In the meantime, it could be helpful if you could find her children and get them here as soon as possible."

Chapter Five

Four Weeks Later

Delilah Morgan quietly closed the door of CC's hospital suite and joined the noisy crowd of doctors and nurses hurrying along the halls. From the looks she was receiving from the hospital staff, she probably looked more like a patient than a visitor. She had just finished another grueling work session with CC. Her thin cotton blouse was soaked with perspiration. Under her suit jacket, the damp material clung to her like a second skin. It was only 10:00 AM but already she was feeling hot, sticky and totally exhausted. Leaning against the wall, she popped two aspirins in her mouth; the dry tablets tasted like pebbles in her throat but she didn't care. At this point swallowing the whole bottle probably wouldn't help. The last two hours with CC had been pure hell. Taking a deep breath to steady herself, she weaved her way down the crowded hall toward the exit doors.

Was it her imagination or was CC's behavior getting worse? Her broken body was slowly beginning to heal, *but* her mental state was in serious doubt; it was one crisis after another. In the past her constant rage about everything was unusual, but these days 'nothing was ever right'; that was

CC as usual. Delilah had learned early in her employment that CC was not a morning person. She usually wasn't civil until much later in the day; some days managing to pull herself together a few minutes before her radio show. Since the accident CC now insisted on early morning work sessions; this was fine with Delilah. Early hours meant she could go home at a decent hour and not spend long days and nights at the radio station. The only drawback to these early morning sessions was CC's new-found rage over her accident and her never-ending sarcastic remarks now started earlier in the day. Delilah felt worn and frazzled before the rest of the world began their normal workday. She sometimes regretted that she had stayed with CC for so many thankless years. Before her accident, it hadn't been too bad, but now, the constant screaming and yelling at every little thing, every workday, was pure torture. The woman was becoming more and more impossible to work for.

Delilah tried to keep in mind that CC had survived a terrible accident. She had not only lost her husband but also the use of her legs. Despite her doctor's best efforts, her severely injured legs were not responding to treatment. Who wouldn't be upset – her entire life had been changed forever.

It was ironic that after the accident, she had rallied the moment, she opened her eyes and saw her room filled with flowers, cards, and well-wishers. Like a queen on a throne, she had held court and basked in all the attention she was receiving. To Delilah, the loss of her husband hadn't really seemed all that important to CC. The only time Robert's name was mentioned was when there was a room full of people or she was being interviewed. Privately, neither Robert Clark nor the circumstances surrounding his death were ever discussed. The attention and adoration that had quickly surrounded her after the accident just as quickly disappeared. The flowers stopped coming; there were no more cards and letters, her visitors had dwindled down to her children, and of course her lowly Personal Assistant. Delilah knew CC well enough to know that the lack of attention deeply troubled her. Overnight Cassandra Clark had become even more angry, bitter and indifferent to the feelings of those around her.

I should be accustomed to her behavior by now, Delilah thought grimly as she dodged a patient being rushed down the hall on a gurney. During the ten years, she had been CC's personal assistant she had been treated like nothing more than a gopher. She had skillfully kept CC's hectic professional and social life in order; along with picking up lattes and dry cleaning on a regular basis. No one knew about the hours of research and writing she had done on CC's column and on her radio show. Her talent had never been acknowledged. Never once had CC thanked her; never once had she congratulated her on a job well done. Why should she bother to acknowledge her? Delilah never complained, never spoke up for herself. It was the perfect setup; the queen and her underling. Delilah had let it happen; she had learned to live with it. "I sound like Cinderella," she muttered to herself as she walked through the electronic doors into the heat and humidity of a typical Houston summer day.

As she stood in the parking lot fumbling in her skirt pocket for her car keys, she tried to put her finger on why today of all days she was feeling so anxious and jumpy. Today's emotional encounter with CC was no different from her usual workday. The minute she walked into the hospital room, CC had started barking orders like a drill sergeant. Her shouting and dissatisfaction with everything was now becoming a typical workday. As usual, CC had compiled a 'to-do-list' a mile long and loudly demanded that Delilah complete the list immediately if not sooner.

"I want this all done today; no excuses," she snapped, shoving the list into Delilah's hands. Inwardly groaning, Delilah looked at the list knowing that at this particular time of day, and the notorious Houston traffic, it would take her days, not hours, to complete each and every item. As far as Delilah could see, there was nothing the least bit urgent or life-threatening on the list; this was just another one of CC's tantrums. Picking up her purse she eased toward the door hoping to escape to a calmer, saner world but her luck ran out.

"Take this tape to the station and see that Ray plays it on the show today." CC held the tape out in front of her.

When Delilah hesitated, CC's eyes flashed angrily, "Keep in mind that I pay your salary; though I wonder sometimes just what you do with the money. You certainly don't spend money on your appearance."

Here we go. Delilah thought, *Criticism of Delilah 101 presented by Cassandra Clark.* The usual criticism began with Delilah's thick glasses and ended with her lack of makeup. It had now escalated to include her hair which hung halfway down her back in a thick brown braid; the grand finale was her poor wardrobe choices. All this criticism she polished off with her usual statement about how she didn't mean to hurt her feelings but was just trying to help her.

Today she didn't even bother to apologize for her rude behavior. She simply turned her back on Delilah and started talking to her daughter Shelby. Shelby was sitting by her mother's bed smiling very smugly as her mother ranted and raved. It didn't really matter to Delilah that Shelby heard her mother's latest put down. Whenever Delilah was in Shelby's presence, she always felt Shelby was looking down her nose at her.

I should have told CC the truth, Delilah thought to herself as she continued digging in her pocket trying to locate her ringing phone. *I should have stood up to her and told her that as of next week the Houston Chronicle will no longer be running her column and that her radio show, which is her pride and joy, has been reduced to 15 minutes of reruns from previous shows.* Delilah gave up the search when the phone finally stopped ringing.

Delilah shook her head. It was sad but CC believed her career was on temporary hiatus; it wasn't. The Cassandra Clark Show was breathing its last breath. The remnants of the Cassandra Clark Show were now firmly ensconced between a smooth jazz program and a program called Cooking with Class. It didn't take a genius to figure out that sooner or later they both would be unemployed. As she continued to dig through her pockets looking for her car keys, her cell phone started ringing again. She tried to ignore it but whoever was calling absolutely refused to accept her voice mail. The phone rang, a minute passed, it rang again. Delilah laid her possessions on the hoof of her car and fished the cell phone out of her pocket.

"Delilah Morgan," she snapped into her cell phone. *My God, she was even beginning to sound like* CC.

"Hi, Dee, are you still at the hospital?" It was Jerry Wainwright, KLS Radio's General Manager. Delilah immediately became suspicious. Where did he get her cell phone number? Jerry had never, as long as she had possessed a cell phone, ever called her. He barely acknowledged her presence; period. He always treated her like a strange creature from another planet. Jerry wanted something, but what? She had watched and listened to Jerry over the years. He always sounded so kind and considerate; that's if you didn't really know him. Those who worked for him knew he would sacrifice anything or anyone for the well-being of KLS Radio. Anyone who had ever worked at KLS knew, without a doubt, that he was known for being conniving and heartless. They also had to concede that he had kept KLS on the air, and at the top of radio ratings in Houston for over forty years. Jerry alone was responsible for CC's rapid rise to the top in the radio world and he always let her know that.

Over the last few months, things had started to change. Shortly before CC's accident, her ratings had begun to slip. Delilah suspected that if the ratings for her show continued to slip Jerry would soon be ready to usher CC out the door. If he thought public sympathy for CC would increase ratings and revenue, he would keep her show on the air forever. If the ratings continued to slip, he would drop the entire show in a heartbeat.

"Hi, Dee," Delilah silently mimicked Jerry. In the ten years, she had worked at the station never once had he called her Dee. Delilah cradled her cell phone between her

face and shoulder as she got into her car and rolled down her car window.

Delilah replied cautiously, "I was just on my way to the station, she lied, I have a few errands to run for CC, but I should be in before her show begins." *Her taped show she wanted to add but kept silent.*

For months the station had been running tapes of CC's previous shows. Like it or not the public was slowly losing interest in the Cassandra Clark Show. If only Jerry would allow her to air this new tape. Whatever was on the tape was new material. It might even renew interest in her show. Delilah fingered the tape in her pocket. Somehow, she had to get Jerry to let her play the tape on the air. While she was convincing Jerry to play CC's tape, she could also solve world hunger, find a cure for AIDS, and bring about world peace. Those three things would be easier for her to accomplish than standing up to Jerry Wainwright.

"We really do need to talk," he said absentmindedly into the phone.

"When you get to the station, make my office your first stop."

He added in a serious tone, "It's important." He hung up without even saying goodbye.

Chapter Six

Two hours later, and two items marked off CC's to-do-list, Delilah stepped into the bright interior of KLS radio station. The lobby of KLS was a beautiful arrangement of fine leather furniture, tastefully arranged on richly patterned Oriental carpets. Discreet recessed lighting set the background for expensive paintings that decorated the paneled walls. Fresh flowers and plants were tastefully arranged on end tables and on the shiny, round mahogany reception desk. It was only if you ventured through the double doors that led away from the lobby that you realized where Jerry Wainwright had saved money. The inter-workings of KLS Radio were so outdated it was small wonder the station was able to send out a signal over the airwaves. CC and Jerry had nice offices. The rest of the staff was stuffed into small cubicles with outdated computers and no privacy. When Norma, the station's receptionist, saw Delilah, she pointed toward Jerry's office making a cutting motion across her throat.

"I know, I know," Delilah said putting her packages behind Norma's desk.

"I'm going to see him right now." She buttoned her suit jacket and adjusted her glasses.

"Do I look alright?"

Norma gave her a sympathetic look that read 'does it matter?'

When Delilah walked into Jerry's office unannounced, he was sitting behind his huge mahogany desk busily typing on his computer. She had never really noticed his office before or his surroundings as she had never been called into his sacred domain. Only a few people at the station were allowed in; a summons to his office meant you or someone who worked there had done something terribly wrong.

Jerry's huge desk took up most of the space in the room. In the corner was a floor to ceiling bookcase stuffed with books he probably had never read. On the walls, bright oil paintings were tastefully arranged. Delilah thought to herself, *if only Jerry had spent a fraction of the money he had spent on his office on the staff offices, morale would be much better. Jerry, being Jerry, he could care less about the staff.*

He knew that she was standing there but he didn't acknowledge her presence. Whenever she looked at Jerry, she secretly wanted to laugh but didn't dare. Five years ago, at the age of 65, Jerry had shaved his balding head, inserted a diamond stud in his left ear, and stuffed his rotund body into an Armani suit. Did anyone laugh; they didn't dare. Even CC hadn't been bold enough to comment on his appearance; at least not when he was around. Whoever was responsible for his dramatic change definitely had a flair for comedy.

Delilah cleared her throat and took off her glasses. When Jerry did swing around to face her, she gave him her best smile; it was false bravado. When he didn't return her smile, she tried to give a look that bordered on defiance. Jerry thought silently, *Delilah Morgan looks ready for a fight. Let's see how she holds up; maybe I've been mistaken about the shy little bird that always seemed to walk a few steps behind CC.*

"How's the diva?" he asked leaning forward and propping both elbows on his desk. He didn't bother to offer her a chair, a glass of water; nothing. The theory that standing and looking down at your opponent gave you power didn't apply to Jerry. Sitting or standing, KLS was his world; he was in charge, he had nothing to prove.

"I'll be perfectly frank with you, Dee; we've just about used up all of CC's reserve show tapes. We've even cut the show down into fifteen-minute segments." He suddenly got up from his chair and walked around the desk causing Delilah to step backward almost losing her footing.

"We're losing sponsorship and listeners by the day. I know CC's been through a lot and she's not in the best of health, but we've got to be realistic; if this downward spiral continues CC's show is history."

Delilah collapsed into the chair facing Jerry's desk. *If this was the end of the line for CC, I will be pushed out the door right along with her.* Delilah frowned and studied her hands; they were starting to shake.

"Jerry, radio is not like television. CC can still have her show. No one will see her. You can revamp the show. When she recovers, she can do her show from a wheelchair if necessary. It doesn't..."

Jerry stopped Delilah in mid-sentence, "Look Dee the station owners have already decided the show has to go. There have been plans in the works for quite a while to replace her with a more current, updated format; this was going on long before her accident." He ignored the stricken look on Delilah's face.

"The show has become old and passé. If you want to know what the rich, the Nuevo rich, and just plain rich and famous are doing you can pick up a hundred magazines at the newsstand or watch it played out on TV. Ever heard of the internet, social media? You don't have to sit by your radio for news. We've got to start appealing to the younger, hip crowd. That's our new direction."

"You're not being fair, Jerry," Delilah countered.

"CC has had the number one talk show in the Houston market for years. She has a loyal following."

"She may have it again, but not at KLS; don't worry we're not going to completely kick her to the curb. We're going to slowly phase her show off the air." To make this point he stood up and swung his arms as if he was taking a golf swing. Delilah could feel herself growing angry. She had to swallow before she dared to let the words come out.

"After all CC has sacrificed for KLS she deserves better than this." Delilah knew she sounded bitter, she didn't care.

"How noble and self-sacrificing of you," he sneered as he sat back down behind his desk. He thought for a moment. *This kid has mocksie after all; the cub protecting the lioness. I wonder if she knows how CC privately mocked her behind her back.*

"If you're so interested in CC's welfare, do this one last favor for her." He leaned forward and laced his fingers together.

"When her show airs this afternoon, I want you to go on the air and give a brief spiel about her health then tell the few listeners she has left that she's leaving the show."

"But Jerry if…"

Jerry ranted on as if he hadn't heard a word she was saying.

"Do you understand, Delilah? This subject is not open to debate."

He checked himself; he was almost shouting. "Maybe, if you play your cards right I'll put in a good word for you with the station owners and you can hang around for a little longer."

The thought of unemployment caused her to tap down her anger. "I've never been on the air before, Jerry; I wouldn't know what to say." She was stalling.

"Cut the modesty act, Delilah, you've been smoothing things over for CC for years. I'm sure you can come up with something. After all, you just said no one can see you. One more cover-up for CC should be no problem for you. Studio B in thirty minutes; you know the drill." He turned back to his computer silently dismissing her.

Delilah nervously fingered the tape in her pocket. "Sure, Jerry, no problem." The thinness in her voice annoyed her and she straightened her shoulders. As she left Jerry's office, Delilah deliberately slammed the office door behind her. It was a small act of defiance, but what did she have to lose? Both she and CC were being mustered out of the KLS army; not even an honorable discharge – just discharged.

Without looking directly at Norma, Delilah retrieved her packages from behind the reception desk and headed for her small cubicle. She set down at her desk and put her head in her hands. She knew what she had to do; but could she do it: As she silently replayed her conversation with Jerry, she thought, *No problem at all, Jerry, dismantling someone's life. I should be a pro at underhanded maneuvering. I've seen the two of you mow people down before; but Jerry Wainwright, I never thought you would ever turn on CC.*

Chapter Seven

Delilah shifted uncomfortably in the large studio chair as they signaled her from outside the booth that there was one minute to airtime. For years Delilah had watched as CC primed herself for her daily show. She usually started her show with a juicy tidbit she had heard at lunch or overhead at the numerous parties and events she attended. When CC was on the air, she used a fake Texas accent. She pitched her voice very low so that people drew in a little closer to their radios waiting to hear what she had to say. She gossiped over the air as if she was sitting, casually having lunch with a friend. Usually, it was harmless gossip; sometimes it was perfectly timed to reveal, devastate, and destroy whoever was not in her favor. To take the bitter edge off some of her attacks she would end the show by imitating Ann Landers and giving out advice that Delilah had typed for her. When Delilah saw the signal from Ray outside the booth, and a bright, red light came on; Delilah knew she was on the air, she also knew she was out on a limb – totally alone. *Here goes nothing* echoed in her ears.

"Good afternoon, Houston, and welcome to the Cassandra Clark Show." That particular phrase she could say in her sleep; now it was bailout time.

"I'm Delilah Morgan, CC's Personal Assistant and I bring you CC's personal greetings, and thanks for your kindness and support during a very trying time in her life." She took a deep breath, trying not to pass out in her chair. "As you all know, CC is recovering in Methodist Hospital, from her automobile accident. She wanted me to thank all her faithful listeners for their loyalty to her and to her show." Delilah took another deep breath.

She pulled the tape out of her pocket and jammed it into the recorder, "But let CC tell you in her own words."

CC's voice flowed across the airways. It was as if she was sitting in the studio with Delilah. Her warm Texas drawl spun its way across the airwaves, as always, charming and seducing her listeners into telling her their most intimate secrets. Her voice heightened in joy as she talked about her recovery and eventual return to the air; it quieted in sadness as she talked about the death of her husband Robert; it was Cassandra Clark at her best. Unfortunately, as Delilah listened, she also had to watch as Jerry stormed outside the studio. He knew he was powerless to stop the broadcast. Cutting her off in the middle of her broadcast would show the listening community how heartless KLS treated a public figure. He couldn't; no, he wouldn't risk bad publicity. No bad publicity for KLS – not on his watch.

I'm finished at KLS, Delilah thought, as the tape rolled on and Jerry continued to pace. She had done the unthinkable; she had defied Jerry Wainwright. No one at KLS ever defied Jerry's wishes and survived to tell about it. Delilah listened to CC's voice and watched the minutes slowly tick off the studio clock. She realized, with horror, that even with her brief message and the tape she still had eight minutes of airtime to fill before the show ended. One line on the telephone started to blink. Jerry signaled her to answer it; Delilah panicked. For ten years she had written copy for CC but she had never had to deal directly with the listening public one on one. She looked up pleadingly at Jerry hoping he would somehow bail her out; with a sadistic smile on his face, he signaled her to pick up the call.

Delilah recognized the caller's voice immediately. It was the woman who in the past had called CC's show almost every day. She had identified herself as LB, Lilly B, or just plain Lillian. CC had handled this caller on a strictly personal basis. The woman had seemed to thrive on all the bad advice and information CC passed on to her. In Delilah's opinion, Lillian must have been a relative or friend who called the show at CC's request to pour out her personal life over the air and ask for advice. Delilah knew from CC's expense accounts that someone with the initials LB had been the recipient of numerous lunches, dinners, and most notable large loans, but she never been able to find out the real connection between the two seemingly different women. To the listening public, Lillian was a woman who had been living in an abusive situation with a mysterious man identified only as Keith. Delilah listened as Lillian droned on and on about the incidents of violence with Keith that recently started to escalate. Lillian asked Delilah to please have CC contact her; she needed help.

As Delilah listened to Lillian's litany of abuse suffered at the hands of Keith, all the hours of thankless research she had carefully prepared for CC reared its head. She thought about the articles and items of interest she researched and submitted to CC only to have her laugh in her face and toss them in the trash. All of a sudden that same information became a loaded gun in Delilah's hand. Delilah spoke softly into the microphone, "Are you employed?"

"Yes, I am," the caller said slowly.

"Does your employer offer as part of the company benefits, a free employee self-help program where employees can get outside counseling? They can actually put you in contact with professionals who are available to handle situations like the one you're involved in. These trained professionals handle everything from drug and alcohol problems to family counseling. You can even get a relationship and grief counseling."

When the caller replied, she sounded angry. "They probably do offer that kind of stuff where I work, but I can't go to them for help; I could lose my job."

"All information is handled on a confidential basis," Delilah said.

"No one will ever know you're seeking help unless you tell them. Perhaps in CC's absence, they can help you…" Delilah paused hoping Lillian would at least consider her advice and hang up.

"Just have CC call me – she'll know what to do." Delilah waited silently praying Lillian would hang up in her face; unfortunately she didn't.

Delilah tried again. "Sometimes one of the hardest things that anyone has to do is give up on someone they truly care about." There was complete silence on the other end of the line.

"You come to a point in time when you finally have to say: 'I give up: I can't live like this any longer; I won't do this anymore.' I believe the term they use now is empowerment. This sense of empowerment over a situation allows you once and for all to say: 'This is the end, I'm leaving this situation for good and I'm not coming back.'"

"It's a hard thing to do; it isn't easy. Only you will know when the time comes to take this step and only you can do it. After you make the decision to change your life, do it, and don't look back. Let me say it again; it's not easy." Delilah could now hear the caller's heavy breathing on the end of the line. The panting sounded as if the caller was going to explode.

Delilah glanced at the studio clock. Just a few more minutes and this will all be over. *Hang up Lillian,* Delilah silently pleaded. The caller stayed on the line lurking in the shadows like a mugger waiting for their next victim. Delilah cleared her throat; she had to get the caller off the phone and off the air before she totally destroyed CC's reputation and what was left of her show.

"Try to keep in mind, it's a given that each day the sun rises in the East and sets in the West. If you stick to your resolve to improve your life and get out of this abusive situation, it's also a given that in time you'll begin to heal. Trust me."

Delilah took a deep breath and imitating CC's best Texas accent she said, "And that advice is According to Delilah. Goodbye, Houston."

Delilah pushed back her chair, grabbed her purse, and ran out of the studio. It was clear to her now; she was finished at KLS but suddenly she didn't care. At this point, all she was interested in was putting as much space as possible between CC, Jerry Wainwright, and KLS Radio. As she ran through the parking lot, she could hear Jerry yelling her name but she didn't turn around. Delilah sprinted across the parking lot and jumped into her car. As she sped through the parking lot, Delilah looked into her rear-view mirror. Jerry was standing in the parking lot waving wildly at her but she ignored him. "You deal with KLS listeners, Jerry, they're your problem, not mine," she muttered in disgust, "They're all yours now."

Chapter Eight

The next morning Delilah couldn't decide whether the ringing in her head was caused by the doorbell or the bottle of wine she consumed the night before. For someone who seldom drank, she had really tied one on. Last night was now a dull, hazy memory. She looked around her small cluttered living room and dropped her aching head into her hands. The pizza box, the empty wine bottle, the wadded dirty tissues littering her coffee table all attested to the fact that last night she had both laughed and cried at the disaster that was known as her life.

After the fiasco at the station, she had walked into her house and listened to the only message on her answering machine. It was a message from CC; short, sweet, and to the point, "I listened to the show today. What the hell do you think you're doing? You're fired!"

After the initial shock of CC's phone message, Delilah ordered the largest pizza she could find and consoled herself with numerous glasses of wine she had kept in storage for longer than she could remember. While she waited for her pizza to arrive she had continued to drink. Her cell phone started ringing and continued ringing non-stop all evening. When she ignored her cell phone her landline started ringing nonstop. In a fit of anger, or maybe approaching drunkenness, she jerked the telephone cord out of the wall. The quiet didn't last long. Her cell phone started ringing again with the annoying song her neighbor had programmed into it. After opening another bottle of wine, she had stopped pouring the wine in a glass, *why bother;* she started drinking right out of the bottle. *Who would be calling her anyway?*

Delilah was sure that the annoying caller was either CC calling to make sure she understood she was fired, or Jerry to personally fire her on CC's behalf. The end result would still be the same, she was fired.

The doorbell's incessant ringing interrupted her thoughts and forced her to acknowledge that it was a brand-new day. Pulling her up from the sofa she shouted, "I'm coming!" Whoever it was had a hell of a nerve showing up at this hour. Her mantel clock chimed ten times letting her know the time of day and increasing the pounding in her head. Squinting through the peephole on her front door she could see the smiling face of Jerry Wainwright. *What does he want?* she thought, opening the door and squinting into the bright light framing his silhouette.

"Good morning, sunshine. Looks like you had one hell of a night." He handed Delilah her newspaper as he brushed past her and walked into the house; a slight smile hovered around the corners of his mouth.

Delilah quickly glanced at herself in the hall mirror as she trailed Jerry into her living room. She gasped; Jerry was right – she looked awful. Her clothes were wrinkled and sweaty from sleeping in them; she looked like a street person. Her face was flushed and her hair was completely matted to her head. Delilah frowned at her image. If she wasn't mistaken, there were even a few pizza crumbs embedded in the thick braid that fell down her back. Trailing behind Jerry into her living room, she deliberately plunked herself down in a chair directly across the room from him so hopefully, he wouldn't pick up the distinct odor of alcohol that clung to her clothes and hair.

Delilah's head was really pounding now. The only aspirin she could remember having were the ones in her desk drawer in KLS. KLS was the only place she always needed plenty of aspirin. Running interference day after day for CC sometimes left her with a headache similar to the one she was experiencing now. Delilah watched Jerry as he tried to find a place to sit on the small, cluttered sofa.

"What do you want, Jerry?" Delilah spat the words out at him. She wasn't usually this hostile, especially with someone like Jerry, but why attempt to be civil; she didn't work for him anymore. Jerry never personally brought good news; it wasn't his style. The good news you would hear from someone else; bad news he delivered himself with a smile on his face. At the moment he was smiling.

"I really wished you had waited after the show, I wanted to talk to you." He removed one of her shoes from the sofa and sat down.

"I tried calling you all evening," he looked around the cluttered living room, "I thought you were out."

Delilah searched through the debris on the coffee table looking for her glasses. She could hear Jerry but she wanted to clearly see the expression on his face.

"After you finished the show yesterday, the phone lines went absolutely wild. People were calling in from everywhere, congratulating you on filling in for CC. The public loved the show." When she didn't reply he rushed on.

"They liked your homespun advice. One listener said: 'It was like listening to an old friend.' You, my dear, are an overnight sensation."

"You're joking," Delilah said cleaning her glasses with the hem of her soiled blouse.

"You know I never joke when it concerns KLS." He leaned forward and offered her his handkerchief; Delilah declined his offer.

"With my help, and of course the station's backing, we have the makings of a damn good radio show and, perhaps, even a new talk show host." He again leaned forward this time rubbing his hands together.

"I can make this happen, Delilah."

He smiled when her mouth dropped open, "Houston's own Dr. Phil."

"You mean temporarily fill in for CC until she returns?"

"No," he drawled, "I mean a show of your own. The audience loved the way you listened to the caller and responded to her. We both know this Lillian character is a nuisance calling CC on the air about some guy who takes pleasure in knocking her around. You didn't string her along like CC. You gave her the cold hard facts and told her to act on them. The public loved it." He pointed his thumb to his chest.

"I loved it." Delilah waited for the other shoe to drop, it didn't take a second.

"What I'm saying in a nutshell, is the Cassandra Clark Show no longer exists. The show is gone – kaput. A show named 'According to Delilah' is a success story in the making. What do you say?"

Delilah was feeling overwhelmed. "I'm flattered Jerry but I don't have the same flair CC had to be a real success on the radio. What she accomplished on daytime radio will never be repeated especially not by me. I just don't have that edge she had to be a real success on talk radio."

"There you go again," Jerry said throwing his hands up in the air.

"Why put yourself down? I personally know that after you came aboard KLS you did most of the writing for CC's show and for her column. CC put her own slant on your words and peddled it to the public. It was always you doing all the real work; you just didn't get credit for it."

"Then why didn't you give me credit for my work?" When he didn't answer, she leaned forward in her chair and did something no one ever did to Jerry Wainwright; she pointed her finger at him.

"Jerry, how can you be so disloyal to CC? She was a success long before I came along. Regardless of what you're saying, she worked hard to make her show a success. That show means everything to her…" Delilah paused; it was time to play her trump care.

"I can't just show up on the air and take CC's place; it just isn't fair. At least give her a chance to make a comeback." She waited for Jerry to play his trump card.

"Dee, the world's not always fair. Here's the deal." It was as if he hadn't heard a word she was saying.

"Be ready at 1:00 today to do another tribute show. If it bombs, we'll both know that yesterday was a flash in the pan. Either way, you play it CC is finished at KLS." He sat back in his chair to let her digest his latest bulletin.

Delilah shook her head in disbelief. "I don't understand how you can write off CC's life and her career like it was nothing. You owe her more than that."

"If anyone owes CC, it's you."

Delilah looked at him. She wished she had the nerve to slap that smile off his face. He was smiling that 'I've got you now' smile. These were the kinds of games Jerry played and he played them well.

He sat forward on the sofa. "Ten years ago, at the ripe old age of 20, you got off the bus from Beaumont, Texas with a college degree in Communications in your hand and no work experience. I don't know why but CC insisted on hiring you. She took a chance on hiring you when I was firmly against it. Now it's your turn to repay her."

He watched to see her reaction. "You're in a position to see that CC leaves the air with the dignity and respect she earned and deserves. You can thank her for giving you a chance when no one else would give you the time of day. If you think about it long enough, you'll realize I'm right." He fired his arrow of reason at her full force.

The arrow found its mark. Delilah squeezed her eyes shut. Her head was really pounding now. She did owe CC for a lot of things, not all of them bad. "I need to talk to CC before I go on her show. I want her to know what's happening before anyone else tells her."

"Well, good luck talking to CC," Jerry said standing up and brushing pizza crumbs off the arm of his suit.

"She stopped taking my calls yesterday. In fact, from what Preston tells me she's not taking anyone's calls."

"I know she'll talk to me," Delilah said following Jerry down the narrow hall to the front door.

"She knows I would never do anything to undermine her."

Jerry stopped and turned around looking into her bloodshot eyes. "And I would?" The statement wasn't said in anger more in mock disbelief.

Delilah returned his intimidating glare. "Yes, Jerry, I believe you would undermine anyone when it comes to the success of KLS."

Her answer didn't surprise him. No apology, no denial from Jerry about his loyalty to KLS. She only wished she had the same loyalty to KLS, but in her heart, she knew she didn't. Delilah stood in her front door as Jerry walked down the front steps and got into the waiting car. He waved as the car drove off.

Standing in the open door she thought, *he never doubts that eventually, everything will end up happening just as he planned. He hooks you like a fish and then he slowly reels you in.* Slamming the door behind her Delilah walked back into her living room, flopped down on the sofa, and stared at the ceiling. *What was she going to do?*

For over an hour Delilah tried to come up with a way to solve both CC and her own problems with KLS. She couldn't take over CC's show without talking to her first. *CC at least deserved to know what was really going on. If I go on the show without telling her what Jerry has planned, I'll feel like nothing more than a traitor.* Delilah argued with herself as she watched her cat Hugo poke thru the pizza crusts that had fallen on the floor. But, she thought, *Jerry had been right.* CC had hired her when no one else would even talk to her. In spite of the way CC had sometimes treated her, Delilah had always been fiercely loyal to her. *Would sitting in for her for a few shows until CC was able to return really be disloyal?* She sat up straight. *My God – was she beginning to think like Jerry Wainwright?*

Delilah plugged her telephone back into the wall jack and dialed CC's private number. She convinced herself, as the phone rang for the fifth time that despite the fact CC had fired her, she still owed her an explanation and an apology. The telephone continued to ring. With any luck, Elizabeth, her housekeeper would answer the phone and put the call through to CC. "Clark residence." Shelby's cooing voice made Delilah sick but at the same time, it frightened her to death.

"Hi, Shelby, it's Delilah, may I speak to CC please?" The 'please' came out in a whine. She sounded like a small child begging for permission.

The sweetness in Shelby's voice was gone; the acid in her voice propelled itself through the telephone line. "Well, if it isn't the new queen of talk show radio. I'd say princess, but you're a little too long in the tooth for that title." She didn't wait for Delilah to answer.

"My mother got the news last night from that slime ball Jerry Wainwright that you're taking over her show; you didn't wait long did you?"

Delilah almost dropped the telephone. Jerry had jumped the gun. Without even consulting her first, he had apparently told CC about his plans for her. Did Jerry think her work was that good or did he think she had waited quietly in the background for the day she would hopefully take over CC's show? Delilah didn't have a chance to answer her own questions. Shelby ranted on; so like her mother these days when things didn't go her way.

"According to Delilah; what a joke," Shelby sneered.

"You'll never be able to fill my mother's shoes. After all, she's done for you the first opportunity that rears its head; you stab her in the back. Well, Miss According to Delilah, my mother is not available. Find some other cripple to kick while they're down; leave my mother alone."

"Jerry asked me to fill in for CC yesterday. It was the only way I could get her tape on the air. You remember the tape she gave me?"

"I remember the tape and I also remember her telling you to give the tape to Ray in the booth to play. There was no mention of you doing the show or personally airing her tape."

"Filling in for CC was Jerry's idea."

"Oh, sure it was," she said sarcastically.

"Good, old, faithful Delilah, always there, always helping out. You're a pathetic substitute for my mother. Let me rephrase that statement; you are pathetic period."

"Shelby, I have always acted in your mother's best interest, you know that." Delilah realized that arguing with Shelby was a losing battle.

"What I do know is that you stole my mother's radio show right out from under her when she was powerless to stop you. Be warned, my mother knows enough people in this town to almost guarantee your failure."

"Shelby, I'm not the enemy. I'm CC's friend; I always have been; I think you know that." Delilah thought she heard a click on the other end of the line as if someone had just hung up; she wondered if it was CC.

"What I know, and what I will let everyone in this town know, is that you and Jerry Wainwright are both lying backstabbers and you've destroyed my mother's career. Don't be surprised if you see me on tomorrow morning's news. Kicking around the life of a defenseless crippled woman, especially a celebrity, will make a very juicy news item. I'm going to make it my own personal campaign to destroy you."

"Shelby, if you will just let me speak to CC I can explain everything." Delilah hated herself for pleading.

The answer to Delilah's plea was a dial tone. She slowly hung up the phone. She promised herself she'd try and reach CC again before today's show. If she didn't reach her today, she'd keep calling until Shelby or whoever answered the phone let her speak to CC. The telephone started ringing again. Delilah snatched up the receiver. Hopefully, it was CC calling back.

The heavy breathing on the other end of the line startled her. As the silence continued, Delilah became frightened. "Hello! Hello!" she shouted into the phone. She probably sounded hysterical to the caller. There was a pause as if whoever was on the line was taking a deep breath.

"Help me! Help me!"

"Who is this?" Delilah tried to sound braver than she actually felt.

"They are trying to kill me. I need your help. They found the phone; they found the phone. Help!" The phone went dead.

"Who is this?" Delilah screamed into the phone. Her only answer was a dial tone.

No caller ID – no star-six-nine. Delilah cursed herself for never bothering to update any of her telephone equipment. She had no way to trace the call, she wouldn't have tried anyway, she was too frightened. Dropping the telephone, she picked up the newspaper Jerry had handed her. Her hands shook as she opened up the newspaper and started turning the pages. On the second page, circled in red, was an article in the middle of the page. Someone had marked the item with a red marker so she wouldn't miss it. The words jumped off the page at her. **"Houston Woman Found Murdered…"**

Chapter Nine

The body of Lillian Barrett was discovered late yesterday afternoon in her southwest Houston apartment. Ms. Barrett was apparently a victim of…

Delilah folded and refolded the newspaper several times before tucking it into her canvas bag. She had read the article at least five times before showering, dressing and running out of her house. A woman by the name of Lillian Barrett was dead. Was this CC's Lillian? Impossible! Had the Lillian who called the show yesterday, listened to her advice and left her abusive situation? *Nonsense* she thought, fumbling with her keys as she locked her front door. It's just a coincidence that the murder victim and the caller shared the same first name. Her head was beginning its familiar pounding causing her to stumble and almost fall as she ran to her car. The question continued to echo in her head, *Was I in some way responsible for her death?*

I have to talk to someone about my suspicions, she thought, as she drove recklessly through the crowded Houston streets to KLS. Before leaving her house, Delilah had called CC but was told by Preston, her son, that she was still asleep. With the exception of her friend and neighbor,

June Irving, she had made very few friends in Houston. Most of her friendships were directly linked with CC. If Shelby was true to her word, she would waste no time getting the word out about Delilah's alleged betrayal of her mother. In a few days she could be virtually friendless. That left only one person to confide in; Jerry Wainwright. Jerry always knows exactly what to do. Over the years he had fixed more than one sticky situation for CC. Maybe, just this once, he would help her, it was worth a try. After all wasn't she the rising new star in the Houston radio world? What a horrible, cruel joke.

Delilah roared into the KLS parking lot barely waiting for the guard to raise the gate. Not thinking she parked in CC's reserved parking space. As she ran past the security guard, he winked at her. He probably thought she hadn't wasted any time grabbing anything that had once belonged to CC. Delilah barreled into the empty lobby surprising her friend Norma, the receptionist, who was calmly answering the busy telephones. Norma hung up from her call and watched wordlessly as Delilah ran across the lobby toward Jerry's office.

"I need to see Jerry right away," Delilah panted as she hurried across the lobby to Jerry's office door preparing to walk in unannounced.

"Jerry's not here Delilah; he left for San Diego this morning."

"That's impossible," Delilah said knocking on his office door to make sure he wasn't there. "He stopped by my house this morning. He can't be out of town."

"He stopped by your house on his way to the airport. He's gone, Delilah." Norma sounded apologetic.

Delilah shook her head. "When I talked to him this morning he didn't say anything to me about going out of town." She sat down in one of the reception area chairs. What was she going to do now?

Norma bit her lip to keep from saying, *"When did he ever consult you or anyone else about his travel plans?"* She held up a piece of paper.

"He left instructions with me on how he wanted things handled while he's gone."

"How long will he be gone?" Delilah stammered.

Not long enough Norma thought silently. "He'll be back in the office on Monday." Holding up a hand to quiet Delilah, Norma answered the telephone.

"Yes, she just came in looking for you. Wait I'll put her on the line."

Norma looked over at Delilah who was sitting in the middle of the lobby slumped in a chair. "It's Jerry, Delilah," Norma said, thinking a *call from Jerry could either make or break your day.*

"He wants to talk to you. Take the call in his office."

At that moment her fondest wish was to sound calm and collected; Jerry hated hysterical women. She failed completely when she screamed into the telephone, "Jerry, she's dead; Lillian Barrett; she's dead."

"Calm down, Delilah. Who's Lillian Barrett?"

"I think it's the Lillian who called CC's show yesterday; she's dead. I think she followed my advice about leaving that Keith character who was abusing her and now she's dead."

"Delilah, for God's sake, calm down…" He paused for a fraction of a second.

"Are you certain it's the same woman? In a city this large there could be dozens of Lillian Barretts. Do you know for sure this is the same woman who was calling CC?"

"No, but…"

"Well, find out before you go running off involving yourself in a murder. It's not good for you or the station."

"The hell with the station," Delilah shouted into the telephone. "A woman has been murdered and I may have been the cause of her death."

Jerry laughed, *what happened to the mild-mannered Delilah he had known for the last ten years?* "Listen to me Delilah and listen carefully. You give people advice; no one says they have to take it. Don't get yourself, or the station, involved in a lot of trumped-up theories about you being the cause of her death. You spoke to the woman one time over the telephone; you told her what she needed to hear. If some lunatic killed her that's unfortunate; it's not your fault. Stay out of this."

He sounded more annoyed than angry. *Don't get involved* was Jerry's answer to everything. There was a long pause as if he was gathering his thoughts.

"What I'm trying to make absolutely clear to you Delilah, is don't get involved in anything that reflects negatively on KLS. If you do, you're on your own." When she still didn't answer, he made one last feeble attempt to pacify her.

"I'll have Mel Houseman, the station's Attorney write up a statement for you to read on the air. If anyone calls you on the air trying to link us with this woman; read the statement and then let it go. Are we clear?"

Delilah waited barely breathing, *Here it comes,* she said to herself, *the old Wainwright snow job.*

"Delilah, you have a very promising career ahead of you; don't blow it on some wasted sense of duty. Don't waste your time and energy chasing down something that more than likely has nothing to do with you. Concentrate instead on making your new show the success I know you want it to be. Don't disappoint all your new friends who have put their faith and trust in you."

She continued listening as Jerry attempted to appease her. Running through her mind were the exact words he had spoken to her earlier. *This station has been my life and I protect what is mine.* That very line was vintage Jerry Wainwright. Protect KLS no matter what the cost. Delilah felt sick. Even if Jerry knew it was the same Lillian Barrett, he would never admit it especially if it brought unfavorable criticism to KLS. If this helped ratings for the station, that was a different story. How could she ever trust him?

He continued on as if nothing she had said mattered. "Next week you and I are going to be meeting with a personal stylist to update your look. We don't want our newest star to look dowdy." He chuckled into the phone.

Dowdy, is that the way you see me, Jerry? Delilah silently wondered; she knew the answer to her own question. Look at her now no makeup, hair still damp from the shower and knotted at the nape of her neck. She had tossed on the first available outfit in her closet in order to get to the station to talk to him. In a few words, Jerry had once again relegated her to a small child with easily solvable problems. He had brushed off her concerns as if they really didn't matter. *Do what you're told and don't ask any questions;* that statement summed up Jerry's rules to live by. Was that how CC had survived all these years? What had she sacrificed to stay in Jerry's good graces? Delilah knew without a doubt, that if her radio popularity turned out to be a 'flash in the pan' Jerry would get rid of two birds with one stone. CC was already gone; would she be next?

Holding the telephone tightly in her shaking hand, she spoke as clearly and calmly as she could manage. If she backed down now, Jerry would probably always treat her as if what she had to say didn't really matter. She took a deep breath and told herself it was now or never.

"Jerry, for some reason, I don't know why, I know this woman was the same Lillian; CC's Lillian. I'm going to find out the truth whether you like it or not." There was silence on the other end of the telephone line.

"If this Lillian is the same person, and I find out that in some way I played a part in her death, then I'll take full responsibility for my mistake, not KLS's mistake, my mistake." Jerry still didn't speak.

"I don't need the station's attorney to write up a statement for me. I'll apologize to the public myself for my mistake and in my own words."

Delilah felt mentally exhausted but she couldn't stop herself. "A woman is dead Jerry. The circumstances surrounding her death are more important to me than what people think of KLS." She slammed down the telephone and stalked out of Jerry's office almost colliding with Norma who had been listening outside the door.

Delilah's face was red as she walked past Norma. "I'm going on the air at 1:00 today to do CC's show. If Jerry calls in and tries to shut me down tell him, I'll either tell my story on KLS or on another station; the choice is up to him." She walked quickly out of the lobby and headed for her small cubicle.

As she passed CC's office, she made a decision. She knew it would be wrong to go through CC's desk but at this point, she really didn't care. Anyone who found her in CC's office wouldn't question her; unless Jerry had already put out the word that no one was to go into CC's office. Surely he hadn't taken the time to issue such an order. Delilah stepped into the dark office, quietly closing the door behind her. Now was the best time to gather any information she could find on Lillian Barrett.

Leave this alone, it's none of your business echoed through her head as she poked and pried with a letter opener at the lock on the bottom drawer of CC's desk. This particular drawer had been off-limits to everyone; including Delilah. The only key to the drawer was kept on CC's keyring. With one final shove, the drawer finally popped open. Delilah hurriedly looked through the dog-eared files that filled the small drawer. She knew time was of the essence. If Jerry ran true to form, eventually he would have Norma go through the office and remove any items that he felt might possibly link Lillian to the station. Delilah looked at the clock. She had less than two hours before she had to go on the air. If she used some of the old research material she had written for CC in the past, maybe she could somehow get through today's broadcast. Who knows, maybe Lillian would call in today alive and well. If Lillian did call in, it would set her world back on course.

Stuck in the back of the drawer was a file marked LB. "This is it," Delilah said out loud, quickly pulling the folder out of the drawer and opening it up. She shuffled through the file hoping to find something, anything that would link Lillian to CC. There was nothing with the name Lillian Barrett in the file. Only the initials LB appeared in CC's cryptic notes. She didn't realize she had been in CC's office that long until she heard Norma's voice over the PA system.

"Delilah Morgan, please report to Studio B." Closing the folder and slamming the drawer shut Delilah left CC's office. As she passed her own small cubicle, she stuffed the folder from CC's office in the canvas shoulder bag that was hanging off the arm of her desk chair. Maybe, after she had a chance to look over the contents, she would be able to link LB to Lillian Barrett; if not, she decided she would take the information to the police.

To her surprise, the afternoon show went off with only a few glitches. Not knowing any gossip Delilah stuck to familiar territory. She had no idea who was sleeping around; who had flown off to Vail Colorado with whose husband, or who was or wasn't invited to the next big social event. She resorted to using her research on computers and the elderly. Delilah managed to use up most of the broadcast on information items. One caller, a widow, who had recently lost her husband after fifty years of marriage filled valuable air time. She was now alone much of the time and was fascinated by Delilah's tips about elderly people who were turning to the computer and internet for news, games, chat rooms, and just communicating with people who shared a similar interest. Delilah warned her of some of the dangers the internet held, but that didn't seem to bother the caller.

Delilah listened as the woman told her about her grandson who was fascinated with computers. The caller thought she would ask him to help her set up her computer and teach her how to use it. Yes, she would be careful; her grandson would look out for her. She was hopeful that maybe this would be one way to keep from being so isolated from the outside world. A widower who had frequently called CC show said he would leave his e-mail address and telephone number with Delilah. If the widow ever felt like just chatting or was interested in hearing about some senior activities in the area, give him a call. Instead of playing this off as a possible romance, or a sinister plot as CC would have done. Delilah encouraged them both to call her after the show and leave their information. She closed the show by providing the audience with the names and telephone numbers of social organizations that had activities for young adults, adults, and senior citizen groups who tried to bring people together with similar interests.

Delilah said to both the widow and the widower, "It's not so much a problem of growing old; the problem is growing old all alone. To all Houstonians, both young and old I say, stay as active as possible, get involved with people and things you really enjoy, and always remember that one is still a whole number. That little bit of advice, Houston, is According to Delilah." She looked through the glass of Studio B and saw Ray standing there with his thumbs up.

As Delilah rushed through the station lobby that Friday afternoon, Norma stood up from the reception desk and shouted to Delilah as she hurried out the front door. "Congratulations, Delilah. I didn't get a chance to listen to your show today, but it must have been really good; the phones are going wild." Delilah walked out of the station without saying a word.

Chapter Ten

Norma used her key to open the entry door to KLS Radio. She had spent last night and most of the morning searching her house for the missing eyeglasses. She was at KLS on a Saturday morning, when she could have been at home sleeping. She took her eyeglasses out of her desk drawer and slammed it shut. *Might as well run my usual Saturday errands since I'm already out,* she thought, as she headed to the ladies' room at the back of the reception area.

Norma pushed open the door and flipped on the light. The reflection in the large mirror validated her suspicion that some repair work was needed; you never knew who you might encounter in the mall. Norma carefully studied her face in the mirror. Her smooth mocha-colored skin defied anyone to guess her age as forty. Her dark braids stopped short of her shoulders and enhanced the youthful image reflected in the mirror.

Pulling a small makeup kit out of her large bag, she brushed eye shadow on the lids of her eyes and applied lipstick to her full lips. She put on her wire-rimmed glasses and blinked at her reflection. While the glasses complemented her large brown eyes and high cheekbones the effect was not that dramatic. *Maybe I need to get some contacts. These glasses spoil the whole picture*, she thought, as *a matter of fact, Delilah could also benefit from ditching her glasses and using contacts.*

Norma was the only African American employee at KLS. Hiring her was Jerry's idea of cultural diversity. She had quietly worked to make herself an integral part of the staff and the go-to person when things needed to be done. Her open friendly manner had made her a person to seek out with their problems, concerns, and secrets. Shrugging off any negative thoughts, she turned off the light and returned to the reception area. As she turned to leave, she noticed the door to Jerry's office was partially open.

"Oh, Lord," she said out loud. If Jerry had come into the station and found his office door open, all hell would break loose. Jerry would accuse everyone in sight of snooping in his office. Everyone's life at the station would be miserable for days, weeks, maybe months. Norma laughed to herself. He would make life miserable for everyone but not her. No, he knew better than to try her patience. There were many times he would have liked to have kicked her out the door but he couldn't afford to. Jerry believed she knew where every bone, body and dirty deal was buried at KLS; but above all else, he knew he could trust her and count on her to keep things on an even keel if he was not in the office or was engaged in one of his underhanded deals. Too bad this supposed loyalty to him was not reflected in her paycheck.

She pushed open Jerry's office door and peeked inside. She fully expected him to be sitting behind that huge desk with that disinterested expression on his face. The only time he was interested in what you had to say was if he had summoned you to his throne room; otherwise, he could care less what you had to say about KLS management.

This would truly kill him, Norma thought as she went around his desk and sat down in his chair. If he came through the door now, he would have shouted, "How dare you sit at my desk."

As she got up to leave, she noticed his middle desk drawer was partially open. Pulling the drawer all the way open she noticed an airline ticket holder. Opening the ticket, she saw that it was a ticket to San Diego. Did he forget his airline ticket? Norma wondered. No that was totally unlike Jerry.

Tucked inside the airline ticket was a business card that read, Horizon Airlines, private jet service to anywhere in the United States. On the other side of the card was written in Jerry's handwriting, the name Jess Stewart and a telephone number. Norma dialed the number.

"Good Afternoon, thank you for calling Horizon Airlines." The girl on the other end of the line sounded like she was twelve years old. Norma thought silently *this is going to be so easy.*

"May I please speak to Mr. Stewart."

"I'm sorry, ma'am," the girl replied, "Mr. Stewart had a private charter yesterday and won't be back until late Sunday."

"Sorry, I didn't reach him before he left. I had an emergency message for Mr. Wainwright." Norma said coyly.

"If only you had called earlier, they were late leaving because Mr. Wainwright's traveling companion was late." Norma could hear the girl typing on a computer.

Traveling companion, Norma thought, *now who was Jerry traveling with? Think fast Norma told herself; find out who's his traveling companion.* "Oh, Miss Lewis is always late; never gets anywhere on time."

The girl sounded extremely young and eager to please. She quickly volunteered the information Norma was looking for. "He's not traveling with a Miss Lewis; the other passenger was a Miss Clark, Shelby Clark."

Norma fell back into the chair. *Shelby Clark. Jerry and Shelby? No, this was not right. Think, Norma, think do you need more information?* "What time are they scheduled to arrive in San Diego?" Norma heard the girl typing on the computer.

"Oh, they're not going to San Diego, they're going to Gaylord. Texas."

Before she could think of something else to ask, a male voice came on the line, "May I help you? Who's calling please?"

Norma slammed down the phone without answering. *Jerry and Shelby flying to Gaylord, Texas; wasn't that where Robert Clark was from? What business did they have there?*

As she left Jerry's office, she tried to pull her thoughts together. *They were probably trying to find Robert's long, lost daughter. If they found Robert's daughter; then what? They would probably bribe her or knock her off whichever was easier. Jerry would probably try to buy her off; he didn't have nerve enough to kill anybody. Shelby, on the other hand, wouldn't hesitate to use harsher means to deal with any problem. When it came to Shelby and money, Norma remembered her grandmother's old saying, 'She'd take a penny off a dead man's eye. Wait until I tell Delilah, this is too good to keep.* With that thought in mind, Norma left the station after closing and locking the entry door.

Chapter Eleven

Delilah spent the entire weekend locked in her house going through CC's file marked 'LB'. She must have checked the locks on her doors and windows a hundred times. Despite the fact she lived alone, she had never questioned the security the house had always offered her. She had always considered the small, square bungalow in the Heights area of Houston as her safe haven; not anymore. The mysterious call she had received, the marked newspaper, the death of the woman named Lillian Barrett had all deeply affected her. Now, whenever the phone rang, she was reluctant to answer fearing she would hear that eerie, sinister voice again. She didn't have to worry; her incoming phone calls for the weekend were limited to her Saturday morning chat with her mother, three telemarketers, and a missed call from Jerry Wainwright.

After going through the LB file several times she found several links to LB that could possibly be Lillian Barrett. Numerous cash payments had been made to the illusive LB. CC had carefully listed each and every entry with dates going back to last year. There were restaurants and out of town hotel receipts that CC had charged to her personal credit cards. Delilah knew that over the past year neither CC nor Robert had traveled that extensively. Some LB expenses CC had put on her KLS expense account, these entries were listed as business lunches. A page from her appointment book had been torn out and scribbled with the notation 'LB has not contacted me personally for three weeks; I hope all is well.' Written in the margin in red was the cryptic note: 'Replace funds taken from Robert's bank account.'

The last payment had been for $200,000. It was a large amount but there was no indication or how the money was used. There were several ten-digit numbers listed that Delilah thought might have been bank account numbers but she wasn't sure. Nothing she read was definite proof that LB and Lillian Barrett was the same person. Maybe the whole thing was just her imagination. Late Sunday night she finally gave up her search for the illusive LB. Stuffing the folder into her canvas bag she decided to turn the information over to the police.

****

Monday proved to be a series of mini-disasters. Delilah had been up most of the night and overslept the next morning. Jerry Wainwright had called late Sunday evening requesting a meeting with her at the station early Monday morning. After his call, she had spent the rest of the night worrying about what he was planning for her. The weather in Houston on Monday morning didn't cooperate. Five inches of rain had fallen before 8:00 AM flooding streets and freeways bringing traffic to a standstill. Delilah had sloshed through water up to her ankles in the KLS parking lot. She had dropped some of her research material in the churning water and as she retrieved it; page after soggy page, the sky opened up again drenching her from head to toe.

Norma on several occasions tried to get Delilah's attention, but Delilah ignored her. On one of the times Delilah passed through the lobby, Norma came from behind her desk and stopped her in mid-flight. In whispered tones, she told her about the information she had discovered over the weekend.

"Listen to me Radio Goddess," Norma said sarcastically. "Jerry didn't go to San Diego last weekend."

"How do you know that?" Delilah asked.

"I found his unused airline tickets to San Diego in his desk along with a business card for a private airline."

"If he didn't go to San Diego, where did he go?" Delilah asked.

"He went to Gaylord, Texas," Norma said in exasperation.

"Isn't that Robert Clark's home town? Wonder why he was going to Gaylord, Texas?" Delilah said in a puzzled tone.

Norma threw up her hands "Beats me Sherlock; that's for you to find out."

When Delilah gave her a puzzled look, Norma smiled and added, "Shelby Clark went with him."

Norma put her finger to her lip, to quiet Delilah when Delilah shouted, "SHELBY CLARK. Shelby and Jerry couldn't stand each other, why would they go anywhere together?"

Norma smiled as she walked back to her desk, "As I said before, that's for you to find out."

****

Delilah thought her head would never stop pounding or her stomach growling as she sat through Jerry's meeting which seemed to go on forever. She met first with the radio station's attorney, Mel Houseman, and signed a short-term contract. The boost in salary alone was a definite plus. She knew she should have been elated, but she wasn't. Something nagged at her; was it guilt? *Shelby and Jerry; what was that all about?*

The personal stylist, Joanna, had come in like a whirlwind promising to make her "the hottest radio personality to hit Houston". "I'll give you a Personal Persona," she promised as she continually circled Delilah's chair gazing in amazement at her wet hair and droopy wrinkled clothes.

Joanna stood in front of Jerry and ticked off a list of hair, makeup, contact lenses and wardrobe then handed the list to Jerry. Jerry balked.

"I turn out a whole product, Jerry, not half." She winked and laughed wickedly.

"Look what I did for you." To Delilah's amazement, Jerry's entire face turned bright red. He raised his eyebrows when Joanna dropped another list on his desk and he saw the total cost for Delilah's makeover.

When he started to object to the cost, she leaned over and pecked him on the cheek. "Just keep in mind you didn't have to spend this kind of money on CC, her husband was

75

a multimillionaire." Clicking her leather shoulder bag shut she strolled out of the office leaving behind a cloud of designer perfume.

Delilah silently wished she had left the office with Joanna. She could tell by the look on Jerry's face she was in for a lengthy reprimand regarding her pursuit of the mysterious LB, she was thoroughly prepared. For a brief moment, they stared at each other across the desk. Never breaking eye contact Delilah finally said, "How was San Diego, Jerry?"

Jerry smiled never missing a beat, "Wonderful; the weather was fabulous. I ate and drank too much, but all in all, I did get KLS some great business."

Liar, Delilah thought, *You never went to San Diego, and what is going on with you and Shelby Clark?*

"How was your weekend, Delilah?"

"I spent most of the weekend trying to figure out the relationship between CC and the mysterious LB."

Jerry held up his hand to cut her off and said sharply, "Leave it alone, Delilah. You have no definite proof that Lillian was linked in any way to CC. Once and for all let it go."

"I do have some proof." She told him about the telephone call and the newspaper.

Jerry laughed. "Some trumped up theories; you call that proof?"

"You're letting your nerves get the best of you. You're going to become a celebrity. Prepare yourself to hear from crackpots every now and then; CC did."

He swung around in his chair and started typing on his computer. He said over this shoulder, "Forget this LB,

Lillian, nonsense and move on." When he turned his back on her, she knew their meeting was officially over.

Delilah had just enough time to grab some of her wet research material and head down to the studio for today's show. She was now more than certain that Jerry knew more about Lillian Barrett than he was willing to admit. *"Prepare to hear from crackpots every now and then; CC did."* Was that a warning?

Luck was with her. Her first caller to the show was the elderly widower, Jack, who had called the show last week. He told her that after the show the widow had contacted him and they had talked for hours. He had invited his new friend to play Bridge with his Bridge Club on Sunday afternoon. She had come to the event and all had gone well. He planned to take her to a play at the Old Opera House in Galveston. He thanked her profusely and encouraged others to get out and meet people. "You meet the nicest people in the most unlikely places." Jack was always so upbeat. He should have been doing a radio show himself.

Before signing off, Delilah supplied the listening audience with the radio's website address. She encouraged them to look at the listing of book clubs, theatre groups, dining, and cooking clubs that were looking for new members. "Thank you again, Jack," Delilah said in closing.

"You're right; you meet the nicest people in the most unlikely places. Get out there Houstonians. There may be someone out there for you, this advice, of course, is According to Delilah."

This time Delilah didn't bolt past the reception desk. To Norma's surprise, she picked up her messages and quietly walked back to her small cubicle. Sitting down at her desk she meticulously recorded Jack Carlisle and Sylvia Brownly's name, e-mail address, and telephone number on her new cell phone. This phone was an updated version CC had given her one Christmas and she constantly used it. She chuckled at Jack's e-mail address. She hoped Sylvia had a sense of humor.

Norma informed her as she walked through the lobby toward the parking lot that CC's children were stopping by to clean out her desk. *Thank goodness I'll be gone when those two show up,* Delilah thought, as she tucked the LB file under her arm and left the station.

Chapter Twelve

The police officer at the front desk of the Houston Police Department looked at Delilah with disdain when she asked directions to the Homicide Department. "Were you called down here," he asked looking her up and down.

"No," Delilah replied. "I have some information on the Barrett homicide. I'd like to talk to someone." The officer raised his bushy eyebrows and shook his head. From what he could see she didn't look like one of those people who showed up to confess every time a murder was committed in the city, but you could never tell.

After a brief telephone call, he informed Delilah, "Detective Marsh is handling the Barrett homicide. His office is on the third floor. Officer Wilemon will meet you at the elevator and give you directions." He motioned to the man standing behind her to step up. Delilah nervously joined the crowd waiting in line to go through the metal detectors then joined the crowd waiting for the elevator.

The overcrowded, air-conditioned third floor, was filled with so many people; Delilah didn't know who to turn to for help. No one was waiting for her. She finally stopped someone who looked as harried as she did only he was wearing a badge. She was relegated to a hard, uncomfortable chair until another officer approached and asked her if the department had called her in, or if she had an appointment. When Delilah nervously gave her reason for being there, he picked up the phone and spoke into it almost in a whisper. The fact that he wouldn't make eye contact with her made her even more nervous.

When he finished the call, he walked with her through the crowded narrow room and left her standing in front of a cubicle. The nameplate on the cubicle read Jordan Marsh. She didn't know whether to knock or go in unannounced. Her dilemma was solved when the man sitting in the cubicle hung up the phone and turned to look at her. He was extremely tall had the most beautiful gray eyes she had ever seen. He smiled and extended his hand.

Delilah didn't know if her difficulty breathing was due to her nervousness or the sudden appearance of the handsome detective. He stood up looking at her; an unreadable expression on his face. Delilah was five ft. eight inches tall and considered herself tall for a woman. She felt dwarfed by this man who was at least three or four inches over six ft. In addition, his slim, muscular build made her acutely aware of her size 12 figure. She compared her plain brown slacks and long sleeve tunic bought off a sales rack at Macy's to his clothes which were obviously much more expensive. *The police must pay much better than KLS,* she thought silently.

He interrupted her thoughts, "Come in, Ms...." He waited for her to supply her name.

"Morgan," she said in a voice she knew he could barely hear. "Delilah Morgan."

"Come in, Ms. Morgan," he said. "Have a seat." He indicated a steel chair in front of his desk. He waited for her to sit down then he sat down in his desk chair and leaned back.

When she still didn't speak he leaned over the desk and said, "Ms. Morgan, I'm Detective Jordan Marsh. You have information on the Barrett homicide." He wasn't gruff, but he wasn't exactly friendly either.

"I'm not sure," Delilah mumbled. This wasn't what she had expected. He wasn't what she had expected. She thought homicide detectives were supposed to be old, overweight, and smoked too much. They were supposed to have seen so much violence they were hardened to the point they were almost unapproachable. Where was the sarcasm, the never-ending cups of coffee, the bad wardrobe? She had been watching too much television.

Delilah knew she probably looked and sounded like she had just made a hasty escape from a mental hospital. "I think I know someone that is connected to the Barrett homicide and may have information about her murder. At least I think my boss may have known her." Delilah knew she wasn't making any sense when Jordan raised one eyebrow. He had been courteous enough but she could tell by the look on his face he had already written her off as a complete waste of time.

She cleared her throat and tried to avoid eye contact with the dark gray eyes that for an instant had turned almost black. He looked puzzled but he didn't take his eyes off of her. He sat staring at her waiting for a surprising revelation.

She had to swallow before she could get a word out of her mouth. "You're probably not familiar with the

Cassandra Clark's radio show, but Cassandra, I mean CC, that's the name she goes by. I'm her personal assistant." Delilah swallowed over the lump in her throat. The headache that had threatened her all day lay waiting to attack her. "Anyway, CC was in an automobile accident a while ago and as a result, I've been doing her radio show."

He leaned forward and folded his hands in front of him, elbows resting on his cluttered desk. "Ms. Morgan, what does this have to do with the Barrett case?"

"Anyway," she said for the second time. Where were the words she was looking for? "Last week the show had an on-air caller named Lillian or Lillie B. I think this same woman had been in contact with CC both privately and on the air for over a year."

"You think that this Lillian or Lillie B is the woman that was murdered last week?" He sounded doubtful.

"I don't know exactly," she said looking down at her hands.

"I think she called the radio station several times asking for CC while I was in the air. Lillian had been in an abusive relationship for the past year with a man she referred to as Keith… She told me the incidents of violence were becoming more and more frequent. She needed to get in touch with CC to ask her for help." He still didn't speak. Delilah nervously pushed her glasses up on her nose and wished she could miraculously disappear. This was not going the way she had planned. She decided it would have been easier to talk to him if he had been an ugly troll; this was even harder than she had imagined.

"I was filling in for CC the last time this Lillian or Lillie B called and I advised her to leave the guy and get professional help. The next day a woman by the name of Lillian Barrett was found beaten to death in her apartment. But you already know that."

"Do you have a last name for this Keith?" He picked up a pen to write down the name.

"No," Delilah replied. "His last name was never mentioned."

"So, you don't know whether this man's real name is actually Keith or if Keith is some imaginary person she made up?"

"Why would she lie about something like that when she knew CC was trying to help her?"

"Why do people tell lies in general, Ms. Morgan? Do you think she was trying to get attention?"

"No. I think she was trying to get professional help."

"Help from an untrained talk show host?" He looked at her in disbelief.

It did sound ridiculous. Maybe she just wasn't explaining it right. "We sometimes can help point people in the right direction so they can get the help they need."

He leaned back in his chair and smiled. "Let me get this straight; you gave a woman by the name of Lillian or Lilly B's advice over the radio to leave some guy that was abusing her. That same day a woman is found dead and you think this is the same woman. You also think the woman was killed based on some nonsense advice you gave her on a talk show?" He ended his long sentence by flipping his pen up in the air.

Delilah caught the pen before it fell off his desk. "I didn't try to give her advice; I tried to point her in the right direction to get the help she needed."

"So, in following your advice you think she got herself killed?"

"I know it doesn't make much sense but I really think this is the same woman I talked to. Here is some information CC had in her desk that might shed some light on the situation. I've tried to make sense of what's in this folder but I can't." Delilah dug into her canvas bag and placed her LB file on the desk in front of Jordan. He didn't make a move to look at the folder.

"Believe me, Detective Marsh, I hope I'm wrong. I hope I didn't give this Lilian person advice that ultimately led to her death."

"What I believe, Ms. Morgan, is that for some reason you've taken some perfectly innocent incident twisted it around to suit your needs and now you're trying to sell it to me as evidence in a murder case." He slowly shook his head.

"I wish I had the manpower and hours to check out all the calls and confessions we've had on this case already. Most of the leads we've received so far have led absolutely nowhere."

"Has it ever occurred to you, Detective Marsh, this could be the lead you're looking for?"

He slowly eased himself out of his chair and walked around to the front of his desk. He towered over Delilah as she sat cringing in her chair. He was even taller than he appeared at first. She didn't look up at him so he leaned down so she could hear him. His gray eyes bore through her like a drill through solid rock. "You're not trying to improve the ratings on your new show, are you?" Delilah looked up dazed as he turned around and walked back behind his desk.

When he sat down, he leaned forward on his elbows, looking directly at her. "Believe it or not I am very familiar with Cassandra Clark. My aunt was a personal friend of CC and also a huge fan. I also know, through my aunt, that you're filling in or taking over her show. For some strange reason, my aunt and Houston have instantly developed a fondness for your new show and its format. But Ms. Morgan, if you think coming in here with some trumped-up story, which you have no real evidence to support, is going to further your career you're sadly mistaken. The information you've given me proves absolutely nothing. However, it's my duty to check out all information regarding this case whether I think it's ridiculous or not."

It was her turn to lean forward over the desk. Delilah. kept her voice and face expressionless. "I'm not trying to improve my ratings, Detective Marsh, I'm trying to help solve a crime. The least you can do is look at the file and see if there is any connection."

The tight smile he gave her, though gorgeous, made her blood boil.

"Let me be the first to say, we appreciate concerned citizens who take the time and trouble to come down and give us information." He reached down, picked up the telephone receiver, and pressed a button.

"Will you come in here please?" He put down the receiver and looked at her. He realized that she didn't fit the MO of the cranks that usually came to the station on a regular basis to provide information on any and every murder case in the city; he had been much too hard on her. He could tell she was only trying to help.

The door opened and a young man stepped into the office.

"Officer Wilemon will you please take Ms. Morgan's statement. She has information regarding the Barrett case." He looked at Delilah with a smile and handed her his card. He quickly picked up Delilah file folder and left the two of them in uncomfortable silence.

Delilah was furious, but she knew he was probably right. Her story at best was so farfetched; she wouldn't have believed it herself. After giving her statement to the young detective she quietly left the police station. It wasn't until she had pulled out of the parking lot that she realized she had forgotten to tell him about the telephone call and the newspaper. *What difference does it make,* she thought grimly? *She had made a complete fool out of herself.* As she drove onto the freeway, she wondered how she could speak and explain herself so freely over the radio but when confronted face-to-face, one-on-one, she always came across as inept. Maybe there was something to the theory: 'They can't see you on the radio.'

Chapter Thirteen

Delilah relaxed in the soft, pale yellow lounge chair and looked around at her plush surroundings. She stretched her arms over her head and flexed her toes; she was in love with life. At 9:00 AM this morning Joanna had dropped her off at a chic spa called Elegance. Joanna had immediately left her in the care of a masseuse named Melanie. "She's the best," Joanna had whispered to her when she saw the hesitant expression on Delilah's face. Joanna had been right. Any tension she had felt before arriving disappeared under Melanie's sixty minutes of gentle care. When Delilah awoke from the series of body scrubs, she was turned over to a very sweet lady named Cindy who had chatted with her non-stop as she buffed and polished her fingers and toes until she was having trouble recognizing them; strange the things she had neglected over the years.

When she thought she was finished, they took her to a hairstylist who began working miracles with her hair. Delilah watched as her long brown braid quickly disappeared. Her hair now barely brushed her slender shoulders. It was a subtle shade of auburn that complimented her complexion. She squinted as she looked at her reflection in the floor to ceiling mirrors across the room. She was still trying to adjust to the contact lenses Joanna had talked her into buying several days ago. She had to admit the contacts were a vast improvement over the thick, black glasses she had worn for as long as she could remember. Wiggling her brightly painted toenails, she smiled. She was now actually looking forward to her makeup session with Kirsten. *Funny*, Delilah thought, looking at herself in the mirror, a few days ago she would have shied away from all this. She would have deemed all of this as nonsense; something she really didn't need… She needed to feel good about herself. *I look and feel wonderful*, she thought as the attendant once again asked her if she needed anything. If these were the perks of her new job, it might not be so bad after all. However, a quiet voice inside her head whispered, *Be careful, if the show's popularity drops, so will your new job with all its perks.*

Delilah accepted the cup of herbal tea and the newspaper one of the attendants handed her and settled deeper into the plush chair. She searched the newspaper to see if they had discontinued CC's daily column. The rumors were true; CC's weekly column had been discontinued. No fanfare, no apology, not even a farewell column to announce her departure. CC had been dropped like the proverbial hot rock. CC had every right to be bitter. First, her radio show was taken away; then after all these years, they have dropped her newspaper column without an explanation to her friends or fans. Delilah slowly shook her head. 'Around Town' now run in the space CC's column had occupied for so many years. Jennifer Holland, one of CC's bitterest rivals, had wasted no time stepping into CC's shoes. Delilah smiled to herself. Writing a society column required connections. It would be years before Jennifer had the same clout as CC. Money and power had been behind CC and had fueled her success. She wondered if Jennifer had taken into consideration the fact that CC had lived in Houston most of her adult life and knew where the bones in Houston society were buried. As a matter of fact, CC had been personally responsible for helping bury a few of those bones. Delilah also wondered if Jerry had read Jennifer's column. If Jennifer became an overnight success, would adding radio to her repertoire threaten her own existence?

Delilah didn't pay too much attention when someone sat down in the chair next to her. However, when she turned and lowered her newspaper she looked directly into the face of Shelby Clark. Both women looked at each other in shock, but as usual, Shelby was the first to respond.

"Well if it isn't little miss According to Delilah. Are you in the salon for a tune-up?"

Shelby looked her up and down in disgust, "You were well past due for some kind of update; you've been dowdy for years."

"Hello, Shelby, how are you?" Delilah replied. *This is going to be ugly,* Delilah thought silently.

"Oh, I'm just fine. My mother, on the other hand, insists upon listening to you on the radio every day then spends the rest of the day crying her eyes out and drinking anything in sight."

"Shelby, I'm so sorry. If you would just let me see CC, I can explain everything to her. You know I call almost every day to talk to her. If you would only let me see her, I know I can make her feel better by letting her know the show is still hers. I'm only sitting in for her until she returns."

Shelby pointed her finger at Delilah, "You are not getting anywhere near my mother; forget it, you'll only make it worst."

"No, Shelby, I know I can make it better: I know I can."

At that moment a salon attendant came into the room and helped Shelby out of her chair. Shelby shook off the attendant's hand and whirled around to face Delilah.

"You are killing off my mother day by day. When you finally do succeed, I hope you can live with yourself. You have destroyed my mother and I will never forgive you nor will anyone else when they finally hear about how you betrayed her. You are a conniving; backstabbing bitch and I hope you rot in hell." Shelby bent down in Delilah's face.

"Oh, are those tears I see? Are those tears for you or for my mother?" She turned and followed the attendant out of the room.

Delilah dropped the newspaper she had been reading. Her hands were shaking so badly she could barely gather up the loose sheets of paper that had fallen to the ground. She got up and stumbled into her private dressing room. There was a button on the wall to call for assistance. She hit the button so hard with the palm of her hand she winced from the pain. With hands she could barely control, she pulled her canvas bag from under the large lounge chair. In frustration she started pulling things out of the bag searching for her cellphone; she needed to call Norma. She discovered she must have left her phone at the radio station.

Delilah sat down on the floor in the small space trying to catch her breath. For several moments she sat clutching her canvas bag to her chest as he rocked back and forth on her heels. She wrapped her arms around herself to stop the tremors that were shaking her body; it didn't work. Her guilt over CC and the murder of the mysterious Lillian overwhelmed her. Delilah continued sitting on the floor, her knees now pulled tightly to her chest. She was overcome by the sorrow that was threatening to completely shatter her. A salon attendant quietly knocked on the door and when Delilah didn't answer gently pushed the door open. When she saw Delilah sitting on the floor with papers scattered around her, she wrinkled her brow and asked very anxiously, "Are you all right, Ms. Morgan?"

"Yes," Delilah murmured, barely able to speak. The attendant looked puzzled.

Delilah started mindlessly stuffing the papers back into her bag. The attendant took the bag out of Delilah's hand and placed it on a chair. She bent down and helped Delilah to her feet. "<u>Kirsten</u> is ready for your makeup session."

She waited a few minutes for Delilah to compose herself then said quietly, "Follow me."

Sheer willpower got her through the makeup session with Kirsten. The joy she had felt earlier in the day had disappeared. She felt cold and empty. All she wanted to do was to go home and go to sleep. She desperately wanted to forget her encounter with Shelby and the guilt she was feeling.

Kirsten patiently gave her instructions on how to apply her makeup, but at the moment she couldn't remember a word she said. She clutched the bag of hair and makeup products to her chest as she jumped out of the makeup chair and headed to her dressing room. Thankfully the spa attendant had finished picking up all the papers Delilah had dropped on the floor and had neatly tucked them back in her bag. Delilah looked at herself in the mirror. Her totally new look all seemed so frivolous; when she thought about what Shelby had said. If something happened to CC as a result of her actions, would the destruction of two people's lives now hang over her head?

Chapter Fourteen

Three Days Later

"You look absolutely gorgeous!" Jerry Wainwright said helping Delilah into a long, shiny limo. "That dress was made for you."

Delilah smiled. The blue sequined long-sleeved dress stopped several inches above her knees. The dress displayed her figure's best advantage. "I have to admit, Joanna knows her stuff, but you already know that don't you Jerry," Delilah said with a knowing laugh. For the second time in her life, she watched Jerry's face turn bright red.

"I feel like Cinderella going to her first real ball. I guess that sounds silly to you doesn't it?"

"Relax, this is just a small party, but it's a way to introduce you to some of the movers and shakers in this town. By the way, the numbers on your show look really good. Keep up the good work." He started to light up a cigar but thought better of it and chose instead brandy from the limousine's small bar. As he sat silently sipping, Delilah saw a chance to talk to him.

"Jerry, about CC…"

"Not tonight, Delilah. Let CC and all your theories rest in peace." He ignored the stricken look on Delilah's face.

"I can't just let it go." She turned in the seat and looked at him.

"It's been over a month and I still haven't heard from CC. I'm really worried something has happened to her. You know CC, if nothing else she would have at least called to tell me I'm doing a terrible job, I've ruined her life; She would say anything to make me feel guilty. Complete silence from CC when she even thinks she's been double-crossed is not her style; that's not CC's MO."

Jerry laughed and sipped his drink. "It's not your fault, Delilah, I've tried several times myself to reach CC by phone but they won't put me through. Her two bodyguards, Preston and Shelby, always give me the same song and dance. 'She's not available; you'll have to call her back.' No one can be asleep and unable to talk 24 hours a day."

"That's why I'm worried. I stopped by the house the other day and they told me she had been with her doctor most of the morning and was unavailable. I just wanted to know if she was alright. They practically threw me off the property."

"You've been to the house to see CC?" Jerry asked in amazement. He smiled.

"Faithful to the end, aren't you?" Delilah fully expected him to pat her on the head like a small dog but the limo stopped at an access gate. A man in a gray uniform came out of the gatehouse and approached the car. Once the limo driver provided Jerry's name, they were waved through the gate. Delilah looked in amazement at the curved driveway and manicured grounds as the car moved toward the house.

The limo stopped and the car door swung open. As the driver helped her out of the car, she stared in awe at the Ashe mansion. How many times had she driven past this great house on her way to work at CC's house? She had often wondered what it looked like on the inside. CC had been a guest here on numerous occasions but Delilah had never been beyond the front door.

As they approached the large double door, the door opened before Jerry could press the doorbell. "Mr. Wainwright, welcome, good to see you again." The woman who greeted them was dressed in a severely cut black pantsuit and very high heels. Her blond hair was pulled back into a bun that served to emphasize her flawless makeup.

"Delilah, this is Tiffany Murray's, Mrs. Ashe's Personal Assistant." Jerry ushered Delilah into a spacious foyer.

"It's a pleasure meeting you," Delilah said extending her hand with a smile.

"This way please," was her only acknowledgment as she led them into a large, crowded room dominated by a wall of floor to ceiling windows.

"This is a beautiful home," Delilah whispered. Delilah noticed that Mrs. Ashe's assistant did not shake her hand when they were introduced nor did she respond to Delilah's comment.

There were several groups of people scattered around the large living room laughing and talking as if they had known each other forever; they probably had. Delilah felt like an outcast. If Jerry hadn't had a firm grip on her elbow, she would have turned around and left.

Jerry handed her a glass of champagne off a passing tray and whispered in her ear. "Go on, smile, and mingle as if this is just another party, and for God's sake let everyone know you're Delilah Morgan from KLS Radio."

He laughed, "Strike a little fear in their hearts, let them know you're CC's replacement and you're not taking any prisoners." When Delilah turned around to object Jerry had disappeared into the crowd.

She received more than a few curious glances from several overdressed matrons who nodded at her but did not make her feel welcome. They didn't know her and they certainly didn't see her as anyone of importance. She spotted Jennifer Holland from the Houston Chronicle newspaper drifting through the crowd; they nearly collided by a small buffet table.

"Gorgeous dress, Delilah, you look fabulous." Jennifer quickly looked around her.

"I almost forgot; we're supposed to be rivals."

Delilah pointed at her. "I'm supposed to hate your guts, after all, you commandeered CC's newspaper column."

"That's right," Jennifer said eating the olive out of her Martini glass.

"We're the two bitches who stole CC's life or so her daughter Shelby has told everyone in town."

"Gypsies, tramps, and thieves, that's what we're known as in some circles. If the truth be known," Delilah said sadly, "they're all relieved CC's gone. Sometimes I wish she would come back just long enough to rub their noses in the dirt."

Jennifer laughed a bit too loudly, "Then we'd both be out of a job."

"Has it been rough on you?" Delilah asked stepping closer.

Jennifer looked over Delilah's shoulder as one of Houston's leading socialites came near the table. Jennifer's smile disappeared as she looked directly at Delilah. "Stay away from my newspaper column and believe me I'll stay away from that pathetic radio station."

She immediately saw what Jennifer was doing. Delilah didn't miss a beat. "Fine and I'll start reading your newspaper column when you cither learn to spell correctly or you worm your way into any significant social events."

The socialite moved in closer, and Jennifer decided to really give them something to talk about. "If you ever want to have something newsworthy to talk about on your show, contact me."

Delilah made sure she was also being heard, "Climb down off your throne, Jennifer, and I'll give you some of the notes CC left me; some of her stories go back decades. You could bring some people in this town to their knees."

"I'll keep that in mind," Jennifer said disappearing into the crowd. The socialite glared at Delilah and walked away.

Delilah swung around to walk away and bumped into a 6′ 4″ wall that she immediately recognized as Detective Marsh. He apologized for running into her and gave her an appreciative smile as he grabbed her arm to steady her.

His gaze lingered a little too long on the bodice of her dress. Delilah knew her face must be red. She silently cursed herself for letting Joanna talk her into buying this particular dress. It was a beautiful dress, but not her style.

"I'm sorry; I hope I didn't spill anything on you." He continued smiling; he hadn't let go of her arm.

"No, I'm fine, thank you," Delilah said stepping back. "But what are you doing here? Are you doing private security?"

He looked puzzled. "No, as a matter of fact, I'm a guest. At least my aunt is a guest. I'm her plus one. I'm the only one willing to go to one of these parties with her. Anyone else would have sense enough to stay at home. I have trouble saying no to my favorite aunt."

"You don't recognize me, do you?" Delilah asked looking up into the gorgeous gray eyes she had seen only once and never forgotten.

He stepped back and looked at her. "No, have we met before?"

I'm Delilah Morgan. The Delilah Morgan you practically threw out of your office about a month ago. He still looked puzzled.

"I came to see you regarding the Lillian Barrett homicide."

He looked as if someone had thrown cold water in his face. "You're that Delilah Morgan? What happened to…" His voice trailed off.

"Don't you mean what happened to you? The last time we met you probably thought I looked like little orphan Annie." She waited for his reply. He looked uneasy as if he'd just realized how he sounded.

"I'm sorry but you have taken me completely by surprise." He put his hand on her arm to draw her away from the middle of the crowded room.

"Your appearance had absolutely nothing to do with what happened that day. I was in the middle of an investigation that was going nowhere. You were in a long line of people who had offered us a lot of useless information and I took out my frustration on you. I apologize."

"Apology accepted," she said shyly. "What you saw in your office that day, Detective Marsh was the real Delilah Morgan." She looked down at her dress.

"What you see now is a version of Delilah Morgan that some days I don't recognize myself—"

He interrupted her. "A version that is absolutely gorgeous." He took a quick sip of his drink and smiled. Delilah was sure her face had turned red again.

"So, tell me, Detective Marsh, have you found any more information on the Lillian Barrett case?"

He frowned. He wished he had even a little good news on that case, but he didn't.

"No, I'm afraid this may go down, I'm sorry to say, as just another unsolved homicide cold case."

Delilah was amazed. She longed to tell him about the telephone call and the newspapers, but she didn't ever want to see that look on his face again when she blurted out her thoughts on the case. "It's hard to believe that the case will just be shoved aside without any real investigation."

"We've had at least ten other homicides since the Barrett case. We have a lot more to go on in some of those cases than the Barrett homicide."

"You would think—" Delilah didn't get to finish her sentence. She was rudely shoved into Detective Marsh's chest as a party guest, who apparently had too many drinks bumped into her.

"Oops, sorry about that," the drunken guest said attempting to wipe the spelled champagne off the front of Delilah's dress.

"Sorry, lovely lady," he said as he started to hand her his handkerchief.

"No, let me get that." H slipped his fingers into the top of her dress as he attempted to wipe the champagne off her chest. Detective Marsh knocked his hand away from Delilah causing Delilah's glass to drop to the floor and break into pieces. The drunk tripped and fell barely missing the broken glass.

Delilah was stunned. Her first party and already she was causing a scene. Several people glanced her way with raised eyebrows. At that embarrassing moment, Delilah realized that the drunk was Preston Clark.

"Preston," Delilah said helping him to his feet, "Are you alright?"

"Yes, I'm fine," he announced getting to his feet and stepping over the broken glass. "Do I know you?"

"It's Delilah," she said anxiously. "Delilah Morgan."

"No way," he said squinting at her through bloodshot eyes. "Not my mother's ex-employee? How are you darling?" He pulled her away from Detective Marsh and drew her to his side. His gaze was again directed down the front of her dress.

"I'm fine, Preston, but, how are you?"

"Never better," he said trying to hold on to her and scrape the broken glass off his shoe at the same time. His fingers were intimately rubbing the side of her dress.

He looked at her closely. "What happened to you? You look like a million bucks. Not like the old days, huh?" He looked around the room.

"Why don't we see if we can find some quiet place to talk and get," he laughed, "reacquainted?" He grabbed Delilah's arm and attempted to pull her away.

"You're drunk, Clark," Detective Marsh said as he pulled Delilah away from him and slipped a steadying arm around her shoulders.

"I don't have to steal anyone's woman; I have enough women of my own." He snagged a glass of champagne off a passing waiter's tray.

They both watched in amazement as he drained the glass. "I hope you're not driving," Detective Marsh said, "I think you may be over the limit."

Preston elbowed him in the ribs, "If I haven't had enough to drink now, I will before I leave this shindig tonight. Good luck with the lady." He started to stagger away.

Delilah caught his arm. "Preston, how is CC? I've been trying to reach her."

"Trying to reach her? Dear Delilah; it's too late to try and reach my mother. She slipped into a world where no one can reach her. In case you haven't heard, my mother has had a complete physical and mental breakdown." His last words were said in a slur.

"What kind of breakdown?" Delilah asked. "The last time I saw her she was fine."

He replied in a singsong voice, "Well, when was the last time you saw my mother? When was the last time anyone saw her?" He laughed as he drained another glass of champagne.

He was past being drunk, now he was angry. "My mother no longer speaks, hardly eats, and doesn't recognize anyone. It's called… I don't remember what it's called," he said scratching his head. "Oh, yes, she sits for hours staring off into space. She's lost in her own world. You're partly responsible you know." He pointed his empty glass at her.

"Don't say that, Preston, I feel guilty enough already." Delilah's voice rose in rising hysteria.

Preston wasn't about to let her off the hook. His loud voice was drawing a crowd, but he was too drunk to care. He again pointed his finger at her, "First my father dies and all her so-called friends desert her; strike one. You take over her radio show; strike two. Then along comes that Jennifer person and she takes over her newspaper column; strike three – final strike. What does the poor woman have left?"

"She still has you and Shelby," Delilah said in desperation.

He laughed loudly. "She can barely stand the sight of us. Do you know what she threatened to do?" He grimaced as a waiter with a tray of champagne flutes purposely avoided him. "She thinks no one wants to be bothered with her anymore; and she's right."

"I call CC every day. I've tried every way possible to see her and explain what happened, but no one will let me near her. If I could just see her and explain what happened," Delilah was almost in tears.

"Well, come on by the Casa Clark, Delilah, everyone is always welcome." He swung his arms to include everyone in the room. His voice was loud and crude.

"All of you come on by and visit my mother for all the good it will do. She won't know you, she won't even acknowledge that you're in the room with her; trust me I've tried." He realized his glass was empty and banged it down on a nearby table.

"When can I come and see her?" Delilah asked somehow hoping he would say, "Let's go see her now."

"How about dropping by tomorrow? That witch Shelby leaves the house for hours every day, doing whatever it is she does. You won't run into her guarding the gates of hell as she usually does. That's what I call the old homestead now; Hell." He belched loudly. "Hell, that word best describes what it's like living in the Clark household these days."

"What time?" Delilah called after him as he weaved his way through the crowd. Preston held up one finger. When he realized it was his middle finger, he burst into loud laughter. He was completely oblivious to the stares and whispers that followed him. If CC could see him now, she would be appalled.

"That guy is a real piece of work," Detective Marsh said, pulling Delilah toward the door. "How well do you know him?"

"Not all that well. He's CC's pride and joy. She also has a daughter, Shelby; actually, they're twins."

"Something has happened to Preston. I've never known him to act like that; especially not in public and especially not to me."

"Just keep in mind when you knew him you probably didn't look the way you do now. He probably considered you then as nothing more than hired help."

"Why thank you, Detective Marsh?"

"Will you stop calling me Detective Marsh, my name is Jordan."

"Well, Jordan, I know exactly what you meant." They both watched as Preston was ushered to the front door by the host.

"I think I better go with you tomorrow when you visit CC."

"Why would you want to do that?" Delilah asked. "I can handle it on my own. Don't worry I won't upset CC by asking about Lillian Barrett."

"Forget Lillian Barrett. I'm not letting you go to that house alone with that maniac on the loose. As a matter of fact, in case that guy is waiting for you outside. I'm going to see that you get home safely."

He quickly looked around the room until he spotted his aunt. "My aunt won't be ready to leave any time soon. I'll drive you home and swing back by and pick her up."

"You don't have to worry about me getting home. I came in a limo with Jerry Wainwright. He'll see that I get home safely."

"This must be your first outing with Wainwright. He'll stay until the last drop of champagne is consumed and the last guest that can do anything for KLS has left for the evening. Unless you want to stay until the wee hours of the morning, I'm your best bet."

"Does the Houston Police Department offer everyone this kind of service?"

"Just doing my job, ma'am," he said as he guided her toward the front door, "just doing my job."

Delilah stopped at the door. "Why are you so anxious to go with me to see CC? Do you think I might not be as off-base about my LB theory as you thought?"

"No. I just want to be there when CC sets you straight, once and for all, that Lillian Barrett and LB are not connected."

Chapter Fifteen

Delilah pulled the pillow over her head to block out the sunlight streaming through her bedroom window. The mantra Today *is Saturday, Today is Saturday you don't have to work today* kept running through her head. Rolling over she desperately fought to seek the oblivion sleep always brought her. It didn't work. Finding sleep the entire night had been relentless. Every time she closed her eyes she saw the gray eyes of Jordan Marsh staring back at her. Forget him she chided herself. So he had given her a chaste kiss on the cheek when he dropped her off after the party; he was just being polite. If she really thought about it she, had gotten better kisses in the dark at a college frat party. Jordan Marsh had probably gone back to the party and picked up someone of real interest to end the evening with; he probably hadn't given her a second thought. Why hadn't she been sophisticated enough to ask him to come in for a drink; a nightcap or whatever it is you do at the end of an evening out. There hadn't been any alcohol in her house since her last ill-fated binge. The only drink she could have offered him was a nice glass of orange juice, iced tea, how about a glass of milk; those were her nightly drinks. She was glad she hadn't offered him a nightcap, if she had, he probably would have laughed at her all the way home.

She pounded the pillow with her fist. She didn't know a thing about Jordan Marsh, but that was her fault. She had been too busy blabbing about her own life; as if he was really interested. He had acted interested or maybe just bored to tears. It didn't matter what he thought, but she knew it did matter. Delilah got out of bed and padded into the kitchen for her first transfusion of coffee. *"You are so anal,"* she said to herself as she noticed that she had turned her coffee maker on automatic and the fresh brew was patiently waiting for her. Putting her coffeemaker on automatic was her weekday routine; why had she done it on the weekend?; you don't have a life was her only answer.

Cradling the hot cup in her hands, she sat down at the kitchen table and propped her feet up on the chair sitting next to her. "Jordan Marsh." She let the name roll off her tongue. It sounded nice. *Is there a Mrs. Jordan Marsh?* She could kick herself for boring him with the details of her life and not finding out one thing about his life; an investigative reporter she was not. He had mentioned that his aunt's name was Jean Phillips. Why did that name sound so familiar? She remembered CC had spoken many times about a friend of hers named Jean Phillips. Was Jordan Marsh related to that same Jean Phillips? Too many questions too early in the morning she thought as she stared into her empty coffee cup. Delilah quickly got up and walked into the small room behind her kitchen; a room she laughingly referred to as her office. She had recently done some research on the Phillips Foundation for her show; she was sure there was a bio on Jean Phillips. She booted up her computer and found a folder she had labeled Phillips Foundation. Inside the file were several old magazine articles on Jean Phillips.

She refilled her coffee cup and then went back and sat down at the small desk. Some of the articles were on the Foundation; others were about Jean's personal life. She read the article about her personal life first. Jean Phillips was an extremely courageous woman who had overcome almost unbelievable tragedy and loss. Jean Phillips had survived adversity that would have brought most people to their knees but she had gone on to do more humanitarian and philanthropic deeds than anyone in the state of Texas. Most of the newspaper articles had been written by CC and chronicled the death of both her sons in infancy; there had been no other children. That tragic event was followed by the death of her two sisters and their husbands in a plane crash a few years later. Tragedy seemed destined to follow her when she lost her own husband in a freak oilfield explosion. She now resided in Houston with her only surviving relative her nephew, Jordan Marsh. Before her husband's tragic death, Jean and her husband had raised Jordan after his parents had died in the plane crash. In another article, CC had written *Jordan Marsh was rumored to be the heir to the Phillips millions, he had chosen instead to join the Houston Police Department.*

Talk about strange; Delilah thought. He's a man of mystery. Everyone I know has secrets. Jordan, CC, Jerry, they all seem to be carrying around secrets; was she the only one in town who didn't have something to hide?

"My God," she muttered to herself looking at the clock on her desk. She was supposed to see CC today; she had almost forgotten. It was 12:00; surely someone was up at

CC's house. She decided to call Preston to make sure he hadn't forgotten he told her she could visit CC today. She hoped last night's binge hadn't erased his memory.

The telephone rang half a dozen times before it was answered. Her only hope was that Preston answered and not Shelby. If Shelby answered the telephone, Delilah knew she wouldn't be visiting CC today.

"Clark Residence."

Delilah couldn't believe it; it was CC's housekeeper Elizabeth. "Elizabeth is this really you?"

"Yes," the voice said hesitantly. "May I ask whose calling?"

"Elizabeth, its Delilah, Delilah Morgan."

"Delilah," Elizabeth said, the usual lilt in her voice… "How are you? Where have you been?"

"I've been right here in Houston. I have been calling you and CC for more than a month. Your home telephone number is unlisted. The last time I called Shelby told me you had moved back to Antigua to take care of your sister."

"Well, don't believe anything that one tells you," she snorted in the phone.

"What she didn't bother to tell you was that without as much as a 'good day' she fired the entire staff. She didn't include me in the first group she let go but she got rid of me later. Shelby and I had a blowout and Shelby told me my services were no longer needed."

Delilah audibly gasped. "You don't work for CC anymore; I can't believe it."

"Well, believe it," she said bitterly. "Shelby let the entire staff go. Even fired Troy; you know how long Troy worked for the Clarks? Everyone who worked for the Clarks was thrown out in the street."

"Are you all right?" Delilah asked.

"Oh, we're all fine. Mr. Clark took good care of all the old-timers in his will; he was more than generous…" She paused and lowered her voice until Delilah could barely hear her.

"The very idea that Mr. Clark left the household staff money in his will really burned up those two ungrateful children of his; especially that Shelby."

"Money's tight right now; that's what Shelby told the old staff. Shelby tried to convince everyone that she and Preston were pinching pennies to keep the house running." Elizabeth snorted again.

"You and I both know Robert Clark had more money than he could ever possibly spend. What burned up those two little brats is the fact he left all his money to Miss CC and didn't leave them a dime; serves them right." Elizabeth talked on almost non-stop.

"So what do the two of them do the week after Mr. Robert's will is read, they up and fire the old staff and hire completely new staff; none of which speak a word of English. That was a smart move; they won't be able to tell what is actually going on in this house. They're too afraid of losing their jobs to ask too many questions or report what is really going on around here."

"What are you doing at the house now?" Delilah asked wondering how Elizabeth had broken down the barriers Shelby and Preston had put in place to keep people out of the house.

"Before Shelby fired me, she asked me if I knew someone who could come in and personally look after Miss CC. I have a friend, a retired nurse, and I recommended her. Shelby hired her on the spot. Well, it seems my friend asked too many questions about Miss CC and her treatment. You can guess how long her employment lasted once she started asking questions. My friend Dorothy Stephen was in this house less than two weeks before she was fired. She called me today to help her move the rest of her things out of the house; that's why I'm here now. As soon as Dorothy puts the last of her things in the car we're both out of here for good."

"I'm supposed to see CC today at 1:00; can you stick around the house until I get there? I'd really like to see you."

"No way am I staying in this house one minute longer than I have to. But listen we can both meet you at the 59 Diner in about an hour. Can you make it?"

"No problem," Delilah said looking at her watch. "I'll be there."

"Good, I have a lot more to tell you, plus I have a letter Miss CC gave me to give to you. I've had the letter for a while. Miss CC said she would tell me when the time was right for me to give it to you. I think that time has finally come. See you in an hour." Elizabeth hung up the phone.

It took Delilah less than an hour to shower, dress, and leave the house. Juggling her keys, purse, and ever-present canvas bag, she managed to get the car door open and jump inside. Putting on her sunglasses she started backing the car down the driveway when she noticed a black BMW was blocking her driveway. Impatiently she blew her car horn. When the car didn't move, she put her arm out the window signaling to the driver she was backing out. The car still didn't move. Slinging her purse over her shoulder, Delilah got out of her car and marched down the driveway. She lightly tapped on the tinted glass window.

"Would you please move your car. I'm trying to get out of my driveway."

The car window slid down and she gasped as she looked into the dark gray eyes of Jordan Marsh.

"Taxi, lady?" He said smiling at her or laughing at her she couldn't tell. Whatever he was doing it was making her mad and very late.

"Look, Jordan, I'm in a hurry, just let me out of the driveway." He chuckled when she put her hand on her hip.

"Get in; I'll take you to CC's house."

"For your information, I'm not going to CC's. I have to meet someone first."

"That's fine," he said reaching over to open the door. "I'll take you wherever you're going."

"I don't need you to take me anywhere, just let me out of the driveway." Was she shouting? Yes, she was definitely shouting.

"Get in the car, Delilah," he said almost impatiently. "I wouldn't want your neighbors to call the cops."

The joke was wasted on Delilah. She got into the car deliberately slamming the car door as hard as she could. If he really took pride in this beautiful, sleek car he probably resented the rough treatment. He didn't raise an eyebrow.

"Where to?" he asked pulling away from the curb.

"The 59 Diner on Shepherd," she replied not looking at him.

"The 59 Diner has the best meatloaf in town but couldn't your date afford a more upscale lunch for the hottest talk show host in town?" He was teasing her and she knew it, but she was angry because he had gotten the upper hand.

"It's not a date," she said louder than she intended. "I'm meeting a friend to pick up some papers."

"Who are you meeting?" he asked not looking at her.

"Jordan, it's a well-known fact that taxi drivers ask you for your destination, they don't ask why you're going there and who you're meeting; stay in your role, okay?" It burned her up that he laughed at her instead of getting mad.

"Secrets," he said in a singsong voice. "Delilah Morgan has secrets."

"You have a lot of nerve talking about secrets. You didn't bother to tell me last night that you are heir to Phillip's fortune."

For the first time since she had met him his whole attitude changed. "It didn't come up, but I see you've been doing your research."

"Don't flatter yourself. I'm doing research on the Phillips Foundation, your name just happened to come up."

"It always does when my aunt is involved." He didn't sound bitter, only a little resigned.

"So, what made you become a policeman when you're the only heir to Phillip's fortune?"

"You're doing it again," Jordan said gazing over at her, "asking questions that are none of your business."

"You've made it my business," Delilah snapped wondering where her bravado was coming from.

"It's a long story, sometime when you're really bored I'll fill you in." He pulled into the parking lot of the 59 Diner. Delilah didn't wait for him to get out of the car. Without looking back, she jumped out of the car and went into the diner leaving Jordan sitting in the car. She quietly slid into a booth and ordered a cup of coffee. She watched through the restaurant window as Jordan got out of his car and walked toward the restaurant.

Stopping at her table, he bent down and whispered in her ear, "So who are we meeting?" He slipped into her booth and ordered a cup of coffee.

"I'm," *she emphasized the I'm,* "I'm meeting CC's former housekeeper and CC's last nurse."

Jordan smiled, "Former and last; looks like CC's cleaning house."

"The woman I'm meeting is Elizabeth Jones, who worked for CC for decades; she's like a member of the family. I can't believe CC's children fired her." Delilah drummed her fingers on the table.

"Elizabeth said Shelby told her funds were running low and they had to cut the staff; that's a lie. Robert Clark was loaded. Elizabeth also told me Robert Clark didn't leave his children a dime; he left it all to CC. So why are Shelby and Preston running the show? Where's CC?"

"Do you think CC's letting them run things now, Jordan asked. It makes perfect sense; I've heard she hasn't been well since the accident."

"I can see you're not familiar with Cassandra Clark. She doesn't let anyone run things for her; she is always in charge. That's what is worrying me; where is CC?"

"After firing the household staff Shelby turns around and hires a whole new staff; most of the new staff doesn't speak a word of English. I have to hand it to Shelby; she is a real piece of work."

"Her brother's not bad either. I think he has a thing for you," Jordan said laughing.

"Preston doesn't know I'm alive," Delilah countered. "I'm here because Elizabeth is bringing me a letter CC wrote to me. If I'm lucky, the letter will tell me what's been going in that house for the past few months."

"You like mysteries, don't you?" He signaled the waitress to bring them another cup of coffee.

"I'm sitting here looking across the table at one big mystery," she smiled and waved her spoon at him.

"The Mystery of the Phillip's Millions." Once again, his total demeanor changed.

Jordan leaned across the table; his gray eyes were glittering orbs of light. "What makes you or anyone else believe that when my aunt dies, I'll inherit all her money? No one ever stops to realize that she doesn't owe me a thing; if anyone owes a debt it's me to my aunt. Aunt Jean and my uncle held my world together when I thought I had lost everything. She doesn't owe me a thing; on the other hand, I owe her everything."

Jordon met Delilah's glare with one of his own. "You want to know why I became a policeman; it's no deep dark secret. After my parents died in a plane crash, the police treated both my aunt and me worse than criminals. My aunt found it hard to believe that on a clear flying day, a plane that was new and well maintained suddenly explodes in midair. My father had always had shady business dealings;

that was no secret. My Uncle had warned him time and time again to change the way he was doing business, but he wouldn't listen."

"The police and the FAA closed the case down immediately. There was no real investigation; it was almost like a cover-up. The police made us practically beg for police reports, evidence, and any information regarding the accident; if in fact, it was an accident. In our case, money didn't matter; they closed us down at every avenue. My Aunt even hired private detectives but they even came up empty. We were shut down and shut out of the entire investigation. Why did I become a policeman, for purely selfish reasons? I decided I would never let another grieving family go through the same experience my aunt and I went through. Nothing will ever bring back the dead, but sometimes knowing a few facts about what actually happened does give the family some closure. My aunt and I didn't get answers we wanted or needed, but maybe I can help someone else find that closure and peace of mind. I may have to deal with tragedy case by case, but I'm determined to do it. Does that answer your question?"

"I'm sorry, Jordan, it was unfair to judge you like that. I apologize." Delilah thought for a moment. "Wait a minute. I can't believe you feel that way after you practically threw me out of your office. Remember I was one of those concerned citizens you were so flippant about."

"Believe it or not, we did follow up on your LB material; it was a dead end. We used your records to check out most of CC's favorite restaurants and hotels, or at least the one she frequented the most. Everyone recognized CC; not so good for the victim. No one recognized the photo of

Lillian Barrett or even remembered seeing CC with her. It was a dead end."

"I wish I could convince myself it's a dead end." Delilah conceded glancing at her watch. Elizabeth was almost an hour late; totally unlike her.

Delilah got up from the table. "Elizabeth must have gotten tied up at CC's; she's never late. Tell you what; drop me off at CC's maybe I can catch Elizabeth before she leaves the house."

Jordan slid out of the booth behind her and took the check out of her hand. "You still haven't given up on this LB thing, have you?"

"No, I haven't forgotten LB and I haven't given up on seeing CC. Somehow, someway I'm going to get in that house and talk to her; they can't keep me out forever."

"Forever is a long time," Jordan muttered under his breath as he followed her out of the diner.

Chapter Sixteen

The temperature was well over 90 degrees with 100 percent humidity when Delilah and Jordan arrived at the Clark mansion. Waves of heat rose from the streets wrapping them both in a steamy blanket of heat. Despite the heat, Preston Clark was pacing back and forth in front of the house puffing on a cigarette and drinking a beer. Whatever had happened to Preston over the last year had taken its toll. Delilah got out of the car and walked up to him as he nervously ground the cigarette out under the toe of his shoe. She hoped the number of beer bottle caps and cigarette butts that littered the driveway were no indication of how long He had been pacing back and forth in the intense heat. CC would have been appalled if she could have seen Preston's total disregard for her home. His personal desecration of the house CC had lived in and loved for so many years would have brought on one of her world-famous tirades. Robert Clark, if he were alive, would have thrown Preston off the grounds immediately. In the last year, Robert had lost all tolerance for Preston and his careless behavior. Delilah had heard Robert threaten, on more than one occasion to disown Preston. Delilah was glad Robert couldn't see his only son now.

Preston stepped in front of Delilah, blocking her way. "I'm sorry, Delilah," he said not making eye contact with her. "My mother won't be able to see you today. This morning has been a complete disaster." He ran his hand through his disheveled hair.

"What happened?" Delilah asked anxiously. "Why can't I see her?" She was working hard not to be intimidated.

"You remember Elizabeth, my mother's housekeeper, well she and her friend showed up here today and really upset my mother." He still would not make eye contact with her.

"That Elizabeth is so ungrateful. After all these years she quits leaving my mother high and dry." His voice softened, "You know how much my mother depended on Elizabeth and she turns around and pulls a stunt like that."

"When she told my mother she was quitting, that nurse friend of hers started spouting off about how we were treating my mother, so Shelby fired her too. No one talks to my sister like that." Preston sounded like a schoolyard bully.

"They scene upset mother to the extent that we had to call Dr. Montgomery to sedate her." He finally looked at Delilah with pleading eyes.

"She's really not up to having visitors today Delilah, I'm sorry."

"You're lying, Preston," Delilah shouted. "I know for a fact that Elizabeth didn't quit; she was fired." Delilah took a step back colliding with Jordan who had walked up behind her.

"How dare you?" Shelby Clark stepped out of the house and hurried down the steps. "How dare you show up here and demand we let you see our mother; haven't you done enough? For the last time, get off our property or I'll call the police."

"You're in luck," Delilah said turning to Jordan. "I brought the police with me."

Shelby looked over Delilah's shoulder and smiled, "Well, if it isn't little Jordie Marsh; how long has it been since we last saw you?"

Delilah looked at Jordan in shocked silence.

"Hello, Shelby," Jordan murmured ignoring the shocked expression on Delilah's face.

"Let me see," Shelby said seeing Delilah's distress.

"Was it before or after mother caught us in bed together that you were shipped to a private school back East and Preston and I were both sent to our own private hell at that prep school in Dallas? Never mind," she smiled wickedly, "let the past be the past, apparently you've forgotten what really happened, haven't you?"

She looked Delilah up and down, "Now you're hanging out with Delilah Morgan. What a shame when you could have had me? I'm a little disappointed in you." She smiled wickedly at Delilah. Jordan was completely silent. If what Shelby was saying was true, Jordan didn't bother to deny it.

"I could care less what went on between the two of you; I just want to see CC." Delilah's voice was beginning to waver. She knew for a fact she was absolutely helpless in a one on one battle with Shelby. At this moment she felt tense and exhausted.

Shelby leaned into Delilah and spat, "You're out of luck and you are not seeing my mother today or any other day. If you think bringing the Gendarmes will get you into the house, you should familiarize yourself with the law. You need a warrant or show probable cause before you waltz into someone's house. Do you or this rent-a-cop have a warrant, Delilah?" She looked directly at Jordan.

"If not, then get off our property and don't come back. My mother is ill, she doesn't need you to keep calling and showing up at her home to upset her. Keep it up and I'll get a restraining order against you." Shelby swung around and walked back up the steps slamming the door behind her.

"I'm sorry about that, Delilah," Preston said backing up the steps. "Shelby is sometimes overly protective; especially with our mother not being able to take care of herself. I promise you'll get in to see my mother but not today." Preston walked into the house and closed the door behind him.

Delilah walked slowly back to the car. She waited until Jordan had gotten in the car and started the engine before she turned on him.

"You didn't bother to tell me that you're well acquainted with the Clarks. So well acquainted you've slept with their daughter. How could I have been so stupid? Of course, you know the Clarks; your families run in the same circles. The only outsider in this group is me. I'm sure if you had shown up alone and batted your eyes at Shelby she would have pulled you through the front door."

Jordan hesitated before he answered. "Shelby embellished that story to upset you; It looks like it worked."

"Jordan Marsh has secrets," Delilah mimicked him in a singsong voice.

"Isn't that what you accused me of earlier; having secrets?"

Jordan rounded on her as he pulled into traffic. "While we're swapping secrets, why don't you tell me what is, or was, going on with you and Preston Clark?" He put up his hand. "And don't bother denying it."

"There is nothing to tell, Preston and I are, were, friends nothing more. He came to the radio station every now and then to see CC and started telling me about a book he wanted to write; he even let me read a few pages. After I started reading some of his material, he started dropping off chapters for me to read; it was really good stuff; that's when we became friends. He confided in me about his dream to move to New York City to do research and write a novel. CC thought the idea of him becoming a writer was laughable. Robert was interested in his efforts simply because it was the first time Preston had ever shown a real interest in anything. With the exception of CC, no one really had the time, or cared, about what happened to Preston."

"But you did care; good, old, reliable Delilah?" They drove the rest of the way to her house in complete silence. When he pulled into the driveway, he took a card out of his pocket, scribbled a number on it, and thrust it at her.

Delilah snatched the card out of his hand and opened the car door. "Preston was so interested in me, he and Shelby left for New York and he didn't even bother to say goodbye. If you think I have, or had, something going on with Preston, other than friendship, you're sadly mistaken." Delilah got out of the car and again slammed the car door as hard as she could. She hesitated, thought about it then went around to Jordan's side of the car and tapped on the window.

The tears that had threatened all day unexpectedly started to fall. As the window slid down and she looked at Jordan, she knew she was about to make a complete fool of herself but she didn't care.

Saying each word carefully she hoped she was getting her point across. "There is something going on with CC and I intend to find out what it is. I don't need or want your help to find out what happened to her; I'll find someone else to help me. Don't worry, I won't bother you again; you're too busy ducking and dodging the truth. You said the police gave you hell when you tried to find out what really happened to your parents; I guess I'm being initiated into that same club. Unlike you, I'm not giving up until I know the truth. In the meantime, Detective Marsh, stay out of my way." Delilah marched up the driveway and into her house.

Chapter Seventeen

Delilah pounded her tear-soaked pillow with her fist and flung the offending item to the floor. It was time to stop feeling sorry for herself and regroup. As much as she hated to face it Jordan, Shelby, even Preston, had made a complete fool out of her. How could she have been so stupid as to trust any of them? Shelby had made her very aware of the fact that Delilah really didn't know Jordan. Jordan had known Preston at the party but had never let her know that he knew him or was even acquainted with the Clark family. He had said his aunt was a personal friend of CC. Why hadn't she caught on then that the two families probably ran in the same circles and more than likely knew each other; that fact was now water under the bridge. Her first priority now was to find out what happened to CC and Elizabeth; both women were missing in action.

As she got out of bed, she wondered how she could get Elizabeth's unlisted telephone number. Other than CC, she didn't know who possibly had Elizabeth's telephone number? She needed to talk to Elizabeth; and above all, she wanted the letter CC had left for her. *Norma!* Norma had once mentioned that she and Elizabeth attended the same church. Maybe, just maybe, Norma had the telephone number or at least might know how to get it.

Delilah grabbed her cell phone off the coffee table and punched in Norma's name It was when she was listening to the phone ringing on the other end that she realized it was past 10:00 PM.

Norma answered as if she was standing behind the KLS reception desk; her voice was crisp and to the point.

"Norma, its Delilah I hope I didn't disturb you."

"No, I just came in from a late dinner. What's the matter Delilah, you sound funny?"

"I'm okay. I need some information."

"What kind of information?" Norma sounded puzzled.

"Didn't you tell me once that you and Elizabeth Jones, CC's housekeeper, attended the same church?"

"Yes, she does. As a matter of fact, we're in several of the same church organizations. Why?"

"You wouldn't by any chance have her home telephone number, would you?"

"What's going on, Delilah?" Norma sounded skeptical.

"Nothing, it's really nothing. Delilah said hesitantly. I was just going to call Elizabeth to see if she had spoken to CC recently that's all."

"You call me at 10:00 PM for an unlisted telephone number; and you tell me it's nothing. Surely, you're not going to call Elizabeth this late. What are you up to Delilah? You don't sound like yourself."

"I'm not up to anything. I just want to talk to someone, anyone who has spoken with CC lately. You know how worried I've been about her. Do you have Elizabeth's number?"

There was a pause on the other end of the line. "Just a minute, I think I have it written down somewhere." Delilah heard her lay down the phone then a rustling noise as if she was sorting through some papers.

"Here it is." Norma read the number off to Delilah.

"Delilah, I hope this doesn't have anything to do with the LB nonsense you've been pursuing," Jerry said. Delilah hung up the phone.

I don't care what Jerry said, Delilah thought, *I don't care what anyone says. I'm going to find out what happened to CC and no one is going to stop me.*

Delilah dialed the number and waited. The telephone was picked up on the first ring.

"Hello," the voice on the other end of the phone was barely audible.

"May I speak to Elizabeth Jones, please?"

"Who's calling?" This time the voice was louder.

"I'm Delilah Morgan. Elizabeth and I, at one time both, worked for Cassandra Clark. I know it's late to be calling but I really need to talk to her."

"Yes, Elizabeth has often spoken of you."

"Elizabeth and I were supposed to meet today and she never showed up. I was checking to see if she's alright. I can call back tomorrow."

There was again a pause at the other end of the line.

"Elizabeth was involved in an auto accident this afternoon. She's in emergency surgery at Ben Taub Hospital. From what the doctors are saying she might not make it."

Delilah almost dropped the telephone. She could still hear the other woman's voice coming through the phone but she couldn't respond.

"Miss Morgan, I'm Elizabeth's aunt, Elizabeth's brother is at the hospital now. The family is gathering here to wait for news on her condition. Please hang up; we're trying to keep the line free just in case my brother calls. Miss Morgan, can you hear me?"

Delilah hung up the phone and buried her head in her hands. What was happening? Shaking her head to clear it, she grabbed her car keys and headed to the hospital.

****

Ben Taub Hospital loomed brightly lit in front of her. After driving around for nearly ten minutes she was able to find a parking space near the building; she parked and hurried inside. The emergency room was surprisingly uncrowded for a Saturday night, but she knew from watching the news that 10:00 PM on a Saturday night in Houston was still early for the largest trauma hospital in the city. Before the night was over every seat and every corridor would be filled with patients seeking aid for everything from gunshot wounds to horrendous automobile accidents. Delilah rushed up to the desk. "I'm here to find a patient named Elizabeth Jones; she was brought in earlier today."

The nurse at the desk punched in some information on her computer then looked up sullenly at Delilah. "She's still in surgery she hasn't been assigned a room." With her pen, she pointed to a man seated in the corner of the Emergency Room.

"I believe that's her brother over there. He might have some new information." Delilah walked over to a slender elderly man who was staring down at the floor rolling the brim of his hat in his hands.

"Mr. Jones?" She sat down beside him. "I'm Delilah Morgan, a friend of Elizabeth. Is there any news on her condition?"

The man raised his bloodshot eyes and looked at her. It was apparent he had been crying when Delilah introduced herself. When he stuck out his hand, Delilah clasped and held it; tears again filled his eyes.

"Elizabeth has spoken of you many times. I'm her brother William. It's so good to finally meet you; Elizabeth thought a lot of you."

"How is she? Have they told you anything?" She squeezed his hand.

"What happened?"

"According to the police, Elizabeth's car went headfirst into Sims Bayou. It was hours before anyone noticed it. By the time they got to the car her friend Dorothy was already dead…" He paused.

"Elizabeth is in pretty bad shape; they don't know yet whether she'll make it."

"I'm sure Elizabeth will be fine; she's one strong woman."

William smiled, "That she is. I'm counting on that strength to pull her through."

"Was it a heart attack or what; did anyone say?"

"Traffic was not very heavy but for some reason, she lost control of her car and it went down the embankment into the bayou. Unless she wakes up and tells us what happened, we may never know. I do know that she had been complaining of headaches but we all put that down to the stress of being fired by CC."

A doctor walked into the emergency room and approached them. They both stood up. Delilah again took William's hand.

"I'm sorry, Mr. Jones, we did everything we could for your sister, but she didn't make it."

William sank into the waiting room chair and again looked down at the floor.

"Thank you, Doctor," Delilah managed to say as she sat down next to William. "Do you have any idea what could have caused the accident?"

William looked up at her with tears in his eyes, "According to the police officer who was at the scene, the car will be towed to a garage and checked for any kind of mechanical failure; it was a pretty old car."

"You can talk to the hospital regarding arrangements for your sister's body," the doctor said slowly walking away. "Again Mr. Jones, I'm sorry."

"I just don't understand," William said, "Elizabeth is gone. It's hard to believe I just talked to her this morning. She was in such good spirits today. She even talked about using some of the money Robert Clark left her to buy a new car and go on her dream vacation."

Delilah squeezed his hand, "Mr. Jones, I'm going to check with a source in the police department and find out the results of their evaluation of her car."

"Will you do that for me, Delilah? It will help give the family some closure."

"I'll find out for you, Mr. Jones. Will you do me one favor? When the hospital turns over her personal effects, will you see if she had a letter for me in her purse or pockets? That letter was one of the reasons she was meeting me today, she had a letter from CC that she wanted me to have."

William looked up at her with tears in his eyes. He squeezed her hand. "If I run across the letter, I'll call you."

She watched him as he slowly walked through the doors of the Emergency Room and out into the humid night air. She followed behind him slowly walking toward the parking garage. Something was happening in her life and she couldn't for the life of her put it all together, but she now had a plan to start pulling the missing pieces together.

Chapter Eighteen

The streets in Delilah's neighborhood were dark and empty as she drove home from the hospital. Her thoughts were completely dominated by all the events that had happened to her in the past few months. The chain of events both excited and frightened her. CC's accident resulting in Robert Clark's death, being pushed into taking over CC's show, the death of Lillian Barrett, and the threatening telephone calls. It was too much to absorb; too much to absorb if you're all alone and don't have anyone to confide in.

When she pulled up into her driveway and got out of her car, she quickly looked up and down the street at all the parked cars to see if she could spot anyone sitting in a car. She had constantly checked her rear-view mirror as she drove home; no one was following her. She rushed into her house, shot the bolt on her front door, and collapsed on her living room couch. What was happening to her? Paranoia, maybe, or was it the fact that in the fifth-largest city in the United States she didn't know a single soul she could call and confide in? She couldn't call Jerry, he would give her his usual speech which amounted to mind your own business, drop this Lillian Barrett nonsense; keep the station out of this. What about Jordan Marsh? NO, she thought quickly. Jordan would listen intently to what she was saying, never indicating one way or the other whether he believed her or not. Norma; she would call Norma. Norma would be annoyed but she would listen.

Delilah dug her address book out of her purse and dialed Norma's number.

Norma's sleep drugged voice answered, "This had better be the Texas State Lottery, Publisher's Clearing House or…"

Delilah didn't let her finish, "Norma it's me, Delilah."

"Delilah, what are you calling me for at this hour?"

"Norma, it's only 11:00 PM."

"Well, Miss Radio Sensation, I have to be at work at 7:00 AM tomorrow. You, on the other hand, can come waltzing in at 12:00 PM or later; well-rested, ready to start your day. I, on the other hand, have been putting up for hours with a cranky individual named Jerry Wainwright."

"I'm sorry, Norma; I called to tell you that Elizabeth was killed today in an automobile accident."

"Elizabeth, who?"

"Elizabeth; CC's housekeeper."

"WHAT?" Norma screamed into the phone. "Was that the car accident on Sims Bayou this afternoon?"

"Yes. I just came from the hospital. I sat with Elizabeth's brother while he waited on the news about Elizabeth's surgery."

"I wish I had known; I would have gone with you to the hospital. Elizabeth was a member of my church."

There was a sudden silence on Norma's end of the phone; then she said very quickly, "Write down my address

Delilah and then come over to my house right now. I'll put on a pot of coffee; we need to talk. In the meantime, I'll call some of my church members. I don't want them to hear about this on the morning news." Before Delilah could reply, Norma hung up.

Delilah drove to Norma's townhome located in southwest Houston in a section called Quail Valley. When she knocked on the door, Norma jerked her inside and asked in a whispered tone, "Were you followed?"

"Who would be following me, Norma?"

"You can't be too careful these days," Norma replied guiding Delilah into her kitchen and putting a hot cup of coffee in her hand.

"Okay," Norma said sternly, "start from the beginning."

Delilah took a sip of coffee and began. "This afternoon, I called CC's house—"

"You call CC every day; what's so unusual about that?" Norma interrupted.

"Today, Elizabeth answered the phone. Did you know CC fired Elizabeth?"

Norma gasped, "CC would never fire Elizabeth. Elizabeth was her right hand; she had been with CC for years. If CC fired Elizabeth, why was Elizabeth still at the house?"

"Apparently, CC's original nurse had been fired and a nurse that Elizabeth recommended was hired. Only the new nurse asked too many questions about CC's care, so she was fired too. Elizabeth had already moved out but she came back to the house to help her friend move out."

"That was the Elizabeth I knew," Norma said sadly, "always there to help someone."

"Elizabeth told me that CC had left a letter for me and that after they finished packing, she would meet me at the 59 Diner and give me the letter; she never showed up. She must have been on her way to meet me when she had the accident."

"So how did you find out about the accident?"

"When I didn't hear from Elizabeth, I called the number you gave me. When I called her house, someone told me about the accident and I immediately went to the hospital. I waited with her brother until we received the terrible news that she had died."

Norma wiped her eyes with a paper napkin. "Something is just not right."

"I know this will sound terrible, but I asked her brother when Elizabeth's personal belongings are turned over to him if my letter is in with her belongings would he give it to me."

"Don't worry your pretty little head over that letter, Delilah. If the letter does exist, Norma will have it in your hands, quick, fast, and in a hurry; rest assured."

"Norma, I have to get in that house and talk to CC; I won't rest until I do."

"The only way you can get in that house to see CC is by breaking in."

"That's might be what I have to do. I have a plan. We…"

Norma held up her hand, "There is no WE, Delilah. Listen to me. I am too old to be put in jail, wear an orange jumpsuit, and eat bologna sandwiches three times a day. Besides, when you get caught, you need me on the outside to bail you out."

"Where would you get bail money, Norma?"

"From Jerry of course," she answered. "He'd bail you out, and no one would ever know; that's what he does for his stars."

Norma looked intently at Delilah, "Ever heard of CC having a DUI?"

"I'm determined to find out what has happened to CC," Delilah said quietly, "and I know just where to start."

Chapter Nineteen

The street where CC's house was located was dark and completely deserted. Delilah knew the area well so the darkness didn't bother her. She smiled to herself as she looked down at the black knit top and black jeans she was wearing. I've been watching too much TV she laughed to herself, but the dark clothing did blend in well with the shadowy surroundings.

Delilah had been very careful. She had checked with Jennifer Holland to see what parties were taking place that evening near or around CC's neighborhood. When cars started arriving outside the secured gates, she carefully got in line. Ed, the guard at the gate smiled at her as she drove up. He had known her for years and didn't question the fact that she was probably visiting CC's house or going to one of the numerous parties scheduled for that evening. She had thought for a brief moment that he would inform her that no visitors were allowed at the Clark house, or ask her who she was visiting. He didn't question her or even write down her license number he just smiled and waved her through.

She found a large group of limos and town cars parked a few blocks away from CC's house. She hoped the valet service that was being used for the parties wouldn't notice her car did not have a ticket fastened under the windshield wiper. She pulled into space behind one of the cars, slouched down in the seat until she couldn't be seen, and waited patiently until the parties were in full swing. When the thick darkness of night finally invaded the neighborhood, Delilah silently got out of her car and jogged the few short blocks to CC's house. If anyone saw her, they would assume she was out for an evening run. Standing behind a tree across the street from CC's house, she stared at the huge, dark, house. She checked her watch. In about three minutes, if she waited patiently, the security guards would ride past the dark house, pause, and then continue on their rounds thinking to themselves that all is well. No one would dare invade this gated, secure community. When the security guards made their rounds, they would see her empty car parked with the other party-goers. She heard the motor of the security car and stepped back into the shadows. The car drove past CC's house, slowed for a moment, flashed lights around the perimeter then continued driving down the street.

As the slow-moving security car pulled around the corner, Delilah crossed the street and approached the house. The wrought-iron gate at the side of the house loomed in the brick wall blocking the entrance to the back of the house.

"Let's see how lazy those children of CC's really are," Delilah muttered thinking how unconcerned CC's children had always been about security. She stuck her hand through the gate and punched in the security code on the keypad inside the gate. The lock on the gate clicked and Delilah pulled it open. She had been right; security in Shelby and Preston's world didn't exist. They hadn't even bothered to change the code on the gate. She silently hoped their carelessness extended to the alarm in the house.

She didn't immediately go into the house. She veered to the right and quietly approached the garage. Standing on her toes she looked into the shadowy interior of the garage to check for cars; the garage was empty. She had been right. Jennifer had told her they both had been invited to Shannon Longwood's engagement party. Preston and Shelby never missed an opportunity to go to any social event. This particular party was being held at her father's hotel in Galveston; so they would be out for a while.

Delilah skirted the pool and walked silently to the kitchen entrance. No need to worry about disarming the alarm now, the house was apparently empty. She wondered if CC had felt well enough to go to the party with them; if so this was her first social venture since the accident. Delilah wondered what CC's reaction, if any, was to the death of Elizabeth and her nurse Mrs. Stephens. Their deaths would have been the perfect opportunity for CC to again appear in the limelight; her grief adding to her persona of sadness that had earlier surrounded her. There had been no words no public comment, no acknowledgment of her personal grief; nothing from CC regarding the death of her former housekeeper who had worked for her for decades. Delilah had learned from Jerry that CC hadn't written, called, or acknowledged Elizabeth's death in any way. Shelby and Preston had made a brief appearance at the funeral. Preston as usual was staggering drunk holding on to Shelby as if she was a lifeline. Delilah wasn't surprised when they both quickly disappeared after the service.

Delilah fumbled with her keys and nervously punched in the security code inside the back door. Luckily the code was also unchanged. The house had kept the same code for as long as she could remember. She had always used the code when she arrived at CC's early in the morning before she went into the station. Picking up CC's daily calendar, sorting her mail, and picking up the numerous messages CC had left her had all been part of her job. CC always had list after list of things she wanted to take care of; Delilah sometimes wondered if the woman ever slept.

When the door clicked open, Delilah crept inside. She hesitated for a moment then decided not to reset the alarm. She would be out of the house before Preston and Shelby returned. She tiptoed through the large kitchen and walked down the narrow hall toward the foyer. She passed CC's office and quietly opened the door. The room was dark, stuffy, and smelled of disuse. It looked as if it had been deserted for years. Papers were strewn on the desk as if CC had just finished working and left in a hurry. Delilah quickly closed the door hoping to block out the memories of the many hours she had spent in this same office with CC.

Delilah stood in the foyer and looked up the gigantic stairway to the second floor. She could almost see CC coming down those stairs to greet her guest. Love her or hate her, CC always hosted grand parties. It was extremely unwise not to attend one of CC's parties; you at least had to make an appearance. CC would give the reason for your non-appearance at her party in her newspaper column. She hinted at the actual reason for your absence from one of her gatherings, but she speculated enough to make you think twice about not showing up at her next soiree.

Delilah climbed the stairs and silently tiptoed down the wide upper hall. From her many visits to the house, Delilah knew exactly where CC's bedroom was located. Before she reached CC's bedroom door, she paused for a moment outside the door of the bedroom CC had always relegated to overnight guests of little importance. Delilah had fit into that category on more than one occasion. This is where the current nurse was probably housed; close enough to be at CC's beck and call at all hours and far enough away not to disturb her. She thought it was wise to check CC's room first. If a new nurse had been hired, she didn't want the newly hired nurse to discover she had broken in and call the police. Shelby would have loved to have her arrested for breaking and entering. It would be a sure way to bring Delilah down. Delilah wondered why there were no lights on; not even a night light in the hall. It was a wonder the nurse didn't run into something if she got up in the night to check on CC.

The door to what was most likely the nurse's room was partly ajar. Maybe the nurse was listening for sounds from CC's room. Delilah gently pushed the door open; the room was empty. The bed was stripped down to the mattress. A bedspread, pillow, and sheets were stacked in a chair as if waiting to be placed on the bed. Delilah walked to the closet; it was completely empty. There was nothing in the closet; no clothes, no shoes; just a set of empty hangers filled the space. Where was CC's new nurse? Surely Preston and Shelby weren't taking care of CC themselves; that was highly unlikely. CC must have gone with her children to the party; they wouldn't have left her alone in this big house.

Delilah quickly left the empty bedroom and walked to CC's bedroom door.

"CC, it's me, Delilah," she said as she opened her bedroom door and stepped inside the darkroom.

"Are you alright? Are you all alone?" Silence filled the large bedroom. Delilah walked over to the bed and looked down. CC's bed was empty; it too had been stripped down to the mattress. Chills shook Delilah's body. Where was CC? You didn't usually strip down your bed before going out for the evening. You wanted that warm welcoming spot ready for you when you returned; a safe snug haven when you had partied the night away. Delilah hurried over to CC's closet and pulled open the doors of the huge walk-in closet. All of CC's clothes were neatly hanging in her closet. The shoes in her floor to ceiling shoe rack were sitting in precise order waiting for her to walk in and make her selection.

Delilah decided to check her bathroom. All CC's cosmetics and perfumes were sitting on a counter. Her hairbrush and comb were lying in a silver tray as if waiting for her to pick them up. Everything was in its exact place. CC must have gone to the party with her children. That was the only explanation. The nurse must have had the night off. There was nothing wrong in this house. Delilah decided she was letting her imagination run away with her. She was just annoyed that she hadn't gotten to speak to CC alone or find out what had happened to Elizabeth and her former nurse. It had been a crazy idea to come to the house in the first place. What had she hoped to accomplish? It was time to stop imagining things.

Delilah backed out of the room into the hall. There was no one in the house, but why should there be. CC had apparently gone out for the evening. In spite of everything, CC had gotten on with her life. Delilah thought maybe she should do the same thing. CC really didn't need Delilah anymore. Maybe she would eventually feel well enough to continue her career. "But not at KLS," Delilah mimicked Jerry. Above all Delilah hoped that one day she would be able to explain to CC that taking over her show temporarily had not been a betrayal. Delilah had always hoped that CC would return to greatness.

Delilah was starting down the stairs when she heard a thud, then a muffled moan. She turned her head in the opposite direction of CC's room. There was a room at the end of the hall that had light shining from under the door. Was someone at home in this otherwise dark house? Delilah walked toward the door and listened. She again heard the moan; it sounded like someone was struggling. Delilah quietly turned the knob on the door and pushed it open.

The stench in the room nearly took her breath away; the smell of urine and vomit filled the small confines of the room. CC was laying on urine-soaked sheets, her hands bound in restraints behind her head. A gag had been placed over her mouth. It was impossible to tell how long she had been there. Her hair was matted to her head and her eyes were the eyes of a madwoman.

"CC, my God, what happened to you?" Delilah shouted removing the gag from her mouth. CC looked up at her with a vacant stare. She didn't speak.

"Who did this to you? I need to get you help." CC looked at Delilah and shook her head. Delilah struggled until she had untied the cotton bands around CC's wrist and released her. She pulled CC up into a sitting position and stuck pillows behind her thin frame. The smell was even worst when she propped CC up into a sitting position.

"I can't, I won't leave you like this. Let me call for help." CC reached out and gripped Delilah's arm. Tears filled CC's eyes. She still didn't speak, but slowly shook her head mouthing the word, "No."

Where was the nurse who now answered the telephone at the house and denied entry or visitation to CC; was she responsible for this? If the nurse was in any way responsible for CC's condition, Delilah vowed she would pay for neglecting her patient. It was hard to believe that either Preston or Shelby didn't at least look in on their mother. She turned around and looked at CC. She sat propped up against the headboard of her bed; her eyes wide and vacant. Delilah smoothed back her hair. CC was almost unrecognizable.

Delilah heard a door slam downstairs. CC's face showed absolute terror; her grip again tightened on Delilah's arm. Delilah heard the voices of Preston and Shelby as they entered the house downstairs. Delilah crept to the bedroom door and stepped out into the hall. They were shouting at each other on the floor below completely unaware that Delilah was in the house.

"Once again, brother dear, you've forgotten to set the alarm." Shelby drawled.

"I have an idiot for a brother; a drunken idiot at that. I don't know who's the bigger drunk, you or that new nurse you hired. You must have searched high and low to find a nurse who has the same drinking habits that you do." Her laugh was cruel and mirthless.

"Before you pass out again, better run upstairs and check on Mommy Dearest; there's no telling what that drunken sot has done to her."

"I'll have a nightcap before I check on mother," Preston slurred.

"That's if it's alright your highness." He laughed as he banged open the door to his father's study.

"Don't think you've had enough for tonight? You can barely stand up. By the time we get this inheritance mess straightened out, you'll have drunk yourself to death. But on second thought go right ahead and drink yourself to death it'll mean more money for me." Shelby laughed a cruel and vicious laugh.

"I have to stay drunk to put up with you," Preston shouted. She could hear the clinking of glassware.

"Do you have any idea…" Delilah couldn't hear the rest of the conversation. The door to the study banged shut. Delilah stepped back into the room and knelt down beside the bed. She held CC's thin almost emaciated hand.

"I'm going to get you help; don't try to stop me. I'll be back to get you as soon as I can." Tears again began streaming down CC's face but she still didn't speak.

"Trust me, CC, whoever did this to you will pay, I promise you." Delilah stepped back into the shadows as the bedroom door opened.

Shelby Clarke stepped through the door and went over to her mother's bed. "How in the world did you work your way out of these restraints? You're stronger than old nurse Hathaway gave you credit." She smoothed back her mother's graying hair.

"I'll speak to Preston, it is not necessary to keep you tied up like this. It's not human." She kissed her mother's forehead. "I don't care what Preston says I'm hiring a new nurse tomorrow to take care of you. This will all be over soon and you can relax and be your old self again. Don't worry I'll always take care of you."

Shelby bent down and again kissed her mother's forehead. She reached over and turned off the light. "Sleep well, Mommy."

Shelby quietly left the room closing the door behind her. Delilah stepped out of the shadows and crossed to the bed. She put her mouth directly above CC's ear. "I'll be back for you, don't worry." CC again shook her head. "I'll get you out of here." CC began to cry in earnest. She mouthed the word "no" but Delilah ignored her. She listened at the door then slipped out into the darkened hall. She could hear Shelby arguing with Preston behind the closed study doors. She silently slipped down the hall and down the winding staircase. She had just crossed the foyer headed for the kitchen entrance when the door to the study opened filling the foyer with light. Delilah had just enough time to slip inside CC's office before Shelby and Preston came barreling out of the study screaming at each other.

"I'm warning you, Shelby, no more. You're out of control."

"I'm out of control? Just look at you." Shelby was screaming. "You have managed to bungle everything I've told you to do. If you could just manage for a moment to stop drinking and think about what's at stake, you'd straighten up."

"I swore after New York, I wasn't going to get mixed up in another one of your schemes but here I am again, involved up to my ass in another one of your hair-brained schemes. I'm sick of it, Shelby, I can't do it anymore. I'm really and truly losing it."

Delilah heard the crack of Shelby's hand as she struck Preston. "Listen to me, brother, we've come too far to back out now. We're both in too deep to back out now. Forget Daddy's money, that mess in New York could put us both in jail for the rest of our lives. If we play our cards right, we get the money, find a nice place for Mommy to stay, then we can go our separate ways. Wasn't that our plan?"

"Our plan?" Preston said. "I think you have it backward: it's your plan. I'm just following the script; the script you wrote."

Shelby's voice had changed from screaming to cajoling, "Listen, baby, I know you cleaned up that mess for me in New York, but keep in mind I've cleaned up your messes for years when you were in trouble. That's what sisters and brothers do for each other. Let's not fight anymore, we need to stick together." The last of their conversation was cut off by the slamming of the door as they both again disappeared into the study.

Delilah silently left CC's office and headed down the hall to the kitchen. She had to get out of the house and get help for CC. She didn't see the red light on the security panel before she pulled open the door. The alarm blared as the door flew open. She heard the door to the study open and Shelby screaming, "Someone has broken into the house." Delilah made it through the back door before a bullet flew past her. The bullet hit the door frame as Delilah ran through it. The wood splintered cutting her cheek, but she continued running. She made it through the back gate as she heard Shelby's voice screaming behind her.

Delilah ran in the opposite direction away from her car as she heard running footsteps behind her; someone was chasing her. She ducked behind a shrub in the front yard of the house next door as her pursuer ran past her. She had no idea how long she sat huddled in the shadows. When she thought it was safe, she walked cautiously back to where she had parked her car. She waited patiently, crouched in her car until several of the guests came out of the well-lit houses down the street and she followed their cars out of the gate. Strange the guard didn't try to stop her. Shelby and Preston must not have alerted the guard that there was a possible prowler on the premises. They wouldn't call the police. Calling the police would draw attention to them; it would draw attention to CC. As she drove aimlessly through the streets, her first concern was how to get CC out of the house before she met the same fate as Lillian. She didn't see the dark sedan that followed her down the street.

Chapter Twenty

Delilah held a handkerchief to the side of her bleeding cheek as she drove aimlessly through the dark streets. She had been driving so long she had become disoriented. Pulling into a strip shopping center she turned off the motor and put her head down on the steering wheel. Where was she? Her surroundings looked familiar but she had no idea where she was. Though everything looked familiar, she was totally lost. What was she supposed to do next? She had tried calling Jerry several times but had only gotten his voice mail. She couldn't call the police; what would she say, "I just broke into the Clark mansion and found its owner tied up in restraints in deplorable conditions. Can you help me?" Jordan Marsh would certainly get a kick out of that.

Jordan. That was it, she would call Jordan. If nothing else, maybe he would forgive her rude behavior and help her find her way home. Her vision was beginning to blur and the side of her face was bleeding. One good thing, she thought, as she dug Jordan's card out of her purse, whoever shot at her had a very bad aim. It must have been Preston; somehow she knew Shelby's aim would be deadly.

She thought for a moment what would she say to Jordan but she had no time to rehearse; he answered the telephone on the first ring.

"Marsh."

"Jordan, its Delilah Morgan." She felt as if she was going to pass out.

"Delilah? What happened? What's the matter, your voice sounds funny?"

"They shot at me. They tried to kill me."

"Who tried to kill you?"

"I don't know which one."

"Okay, stay calm. Tell me where you are."

"I don't know where I am." She dabbed at her bleeding cheek and started to cry.

"Are you in your car?"

"Yes, but I'm parked in a strip center."

"Delilah, are you hurt?"

"They shot at me, my face is bleeding."

"Stay calm. Look out your window. Do you see a store; a street sign, anything?"

"Looking out my car window across the street I see a hardware store."

"What's the name of the store? Can you see it?"

"Fuller Hardware & Supply."

"Don't move, I'll be right there." He hung up before she could answer.

Ten minutes later a black BMW pulled into the parking space next to her. Delilah got out of her car and the last thing she remembered was Jordan Marsh catching her as she fell to the pavement.

"Drink this, dear, it will make you feel better." Delilah didn't recognize the voice. All she knew was the voice was a woman's and it was soft and soothing.

She looked around but didn't recognize her surroundings. She touched her face, a bandage had been placed on her cheek but the pain in her face still remained.

"Don't touch that now." A reassuring hand brushed her cheek. "Your face was grazed by something; a piece of wood I think."

"Who are you?" Delilah asked as she attempted to sit up.

"I'm Jean Phillips and you are…?"

"Delilah, Delilah Morgan," Jordan answered as he walked into the room. "The Delilah Morgan from the famous or infamous 'According to Delilah Show'."

"No time to be sarcastic, Jordan," Jean said easing Delilah back on the sofa and tucking a blanket around her.

"Just for curiosity's sake, Delilah," Jordan said, sitting down across from her, "who shot at you?"

"It was either Shelby or Preston Clark, I don't know which one." Delilah's head was pounding so hard she could barely see.

"What did you do storm the Clark house to see CC or was it just plain breaking and entering?" Jordan's voice sounded both concerned and amused.

When Delilah didn't answer, he slowly shook his head.

"Give her a chance to speak, Jordan, she seems to have been through a lot. Give her a chance to get her bearings."

Jordan looked at Delilah and his tone softened. "Okay, tell us what happened. I know you must have been truly desperate to call me. What happened and don't leave anything out."

Delilah laid back on the soft pillows and told them about her ill-fated attempt to see CC.

"I found her. I found CC, but it wasn't what I had expected. She was tied up in the house and left virtually alone with no one to care for her. I need to get her out of that house. You've got to help me."

"She was tied up?" Jean Phillips looked at Delilah. "CC was tied to her bed and left there? I can't believe this. I knew there were problems with CC and her children lately but I never would have believed they would treat her like that. Something is not right."

Jean Phillips got to her feet. "I'm going over there right now and get her out of there. Let either one of her children try to stop me. If either one of them wants to start shooting."

Jean opened a desk drawer and drew out a large pistol. "Bring 'em on."

Jordan took the gun out of his aunt's hand. "Before you go over there Annie Oakley, let me make a few calls. If what Delilah says is true and CC's life is in danger, we can make a welfare call and get her out of there; but for crying out loud let's do it legally." He finished his sentence by slamming the desk drawer shut.

"I don't care how we do it; we need to get her out of there tonight." Delilah threw aside the blanket and started to get up.

"Delilah, if you go over there now demanding to get CC out of the house they're going to know you were the one who broke in. We might get CC out of the house but you could be arrested for breaking and entering. Let me handle this," Jordan said sternly.

Before Jean could answer, Jordan's cell phone rang and he turned and left the room to take the call. Jean again attempted to make Delilah lie down but Delilah refused. She was fired up now; her mission was to get CC out of her house.

Jordan was putting on his jacket and putting his cell phone in his pocket when he came back into the room.

"I don't have details yet, but apparently something has happened at CC's house. I'm on my way over there now."

"Both of you," he pointed his finger at Delilah and Jean, "please stay put."

Delilah was already on her feet. "What happened at CC's, tell me."

Jordan did not make eye contact with her. "I've got to go, he said over his shoulder."

"I'm going with you and don't try to stop me." Delilah put on her shoes and grabbed her purse.

"This is police business, Delilah. You'll have to wait here."

"Not on your life," Delilah said angrily. "If it involves CC, I'm going with you." Delilah stood up and followed Jordan out of the room.

Shaking his head, Jordan put his hand on her shoulder. "You want to run the risk of being arrested?"

"I want to run the risk of saving my friend. I promise I'll wait in the car. Please Jordan, let me go with you."

"Okay, but I want your word you'll stay in the car. If Shelby or Preston sees you, they might put two and two together and figure out it was you who broke into the house."

"I promise I'll stay in the car. Let's go."

****

Delilah sat in the car and watched as Jordan crossed the street and walked up the driveway to CC's house. There were two police cars parked in the driveway. Two police officers met Jordan and he immediately followed them to the back of the house. Time seems to crawl by; no sign of Jordan. Delilah got out of the car and crossed the street. She stood behind one of the police cars, out of sight, looking for Jordan. In the distance, she could hear sirens approaching the house. She dashed around the side of the house trying to keep out of sight. She saw Jordan and the two police officers huddled together in a small group. When they stepped aside she saw what they had been looking at. The body of Cassandra Clark floated face down in the huge swimming pool.

Chapter Twenty-One

From behind her sunglasses, Delilah scanned the crowd that had gathered at CC's gravesite. She was surprised at the size of the crowd and the total lack of emotion displayed not only by CC's children but the entire crowd. As the crowd began to disburse, she noticed three women who genuinely seemed to at least mourn CC's passing. The heavy makeup and pink spiked hair on one of the women was a clear indication to Delilah that these were probably not people CC would normally know or acknowledge. Slowly working her way through the crowd toward them Delilah heard part of their conversation.

"When Lillian started occasionally doing CC's hair, she put us on the map. I don't know whether she blackmailed some of her friends or not into coming to the shop but whatever she did business went through the roof."

The one-woman without the colorful hair looked at the other two and smiled. "I personally think it was the daughter that brought in the crowd. After CC physically drug her daughter into the salon, the daughter left satisfied, that's when the business really started to pick up. I think that pain in the ass daughter of hers was the start of the young trendy crowd coming to the salon; too bad it didn't last."

Delilah stepped into the middle of their conversation. "You knew Lillian Barrett?"

Pinked spiked hair put her hand on her hip, "Who wants to know?"

"I'm Delilah Morgan, I'm temporarily taking over CC's show."

Pink spiked hair looked Delilah up and down. "Yeah, I listened to your show a couple of times until you stopped dishing out gossip on the rich and famous and starting catering to senior citizens. Boring." The three women turned and started to walk away.

Delilah walked behind them. She had to think of a way to talk to these three about Lillian and her connection to CC. "I was thinking that perhaps if you offered a half-priced day early in the week for senior clients, I could advertise it on the air, free of charge, of course, it may boost your business again. Here's my card. Get in contact with me if you are interested."

One of the women turned around and walked back toward her extending her hand. "I'm Nora Fleming, owner of Short Cuts Hair Salon. We'll be in touch."

"I'm in," Delilah muttered to herself as she walked through the crowd looking for Jerry. *Don't worry CC, I'll find out what really happened to you.*

****

"What in the world were you thinking?" Jerry yelled as he walked into Delilah's office. "You gave free advertising to," he looked at the paper in his hand, "Short Cut Hair Salon. In case you haven't noticed Delilah, this station depends on paid advertising. We don't give it away for free."

"It was a one-time thing, Jerry; I don't think the station will go broke. Maybe now since I've broken one of your many rules, you'll accept my resignation from KLS."

"Oh, here we go again." He threw the papers in his hands-on Delilah's desk. "I'll remind you as I often had to remind CC, you break your contract with the station and walk out the door I'll sue you for breach of contract and make sure the only job you get in this town will be sweeping up hair at Short Cut Hair Salon."

"What's happened to the meek and mild-mannered Delilah Morgan who always walked in CC's shadow? All of a sudden, just like CC, you think you've become so powerful you can walk over me and everyone else who crosses your path. Well, it won't happen. Keep that in mind."

"Is that how you kept CC in line, Jerry, with threats? Keep in mind I never wanted this job in the first place, you forced me into it…" Before he could answer, Jerry turned to leave Delilah's office.

"How I kept CC in line is none of your business…" He paused in her doorway.

"No more free advertising, got that." He slammed the door behind him.

****

Delilah stepped into the cool interior of the Short Cut Salon. It was really more than she expected. The plush furniture, gleaming hardwood floors, wall artwork, and soft music were all designed to provide a relaxing stress-free environment. The lady with the Pink Tipped Hair got out of her salon chair when she saw Delilah and walked toward her with an outstretched hand.

"I don't know whether to kiss you or kill you."

Delilah looked at her in surprise. "What happened?"

"Come on back to the break room and I'll fill you in. Oh, and by the way my name is Lauren."

Delilah sat down at a small table in the break room and Lauren placed a glass of iced tea in front of her.

"That little senior citizen commercial you did last Friday for our salon announcing our half-price specials on Tuesday. Well, those gals came piling in here like gangbusters on Tuesday and we finally had to close the doors. But you know what, they were very patient, waited their turn and showed a real appreciation for our work; I liked that. As a matter of fact, Nora is looking into the empty space next door to expand the business; More chairs, more operators; the sky is the limit."

"I'm glad things worked out for you, but that's not why I'm here."

"I figured that. What do you want?"

"I want some information on Lillian Barrett."

"Humph. For your information, there is no Lillian Barrett. Her real name was Lillian Stewart. Why she made up that name is a mystery to me; but she did. All of her identification, driver's license, bank accounts, credit cards, even her beautician license were in the name of Lillian Stewart."

Delilah moved closer to her. "How do you know all of this?"

"When Lillian first moved to Houston, she went from hair salon to hair salon looking for a booth to rent. One of my friends in another salon told her about us and when she came in Nora hired her. Talk about being down on her luck; she was really hitting rock bottom. She confided in me that she was living in one of those weekly rental motels, but she was fast running out of money. She was a top-notch stylist in New Your but she hadn't built up her client list in Houston so she was operating on a wing and a prayer."

She sipped her drink and continued "Fool that I am I let her crash at my place so she could save some money and get back on her feet."

"How long did she stay with you?" Delilah asked wishing that she could write down some of this information without looking suspicious.

"Here's the funny thing, one day Cassandra Clark shows up at the salon and Lillian did her hair. They put their heads together and whispered to each other. When Miss Clark left, her hair looked great but she looked nervous and very irritated. I asked Lillian about it but she said they got into an argument over politics. Lillian discussing politics; that's a joke right there. A couple of days later, Lillian came to work driving a brand-new car. This girl who barely had two nickels to rub together gets a brand-new car and on top of that pays a month's rent on my apartment. Two weeks later she packed her bags and left my apartment without a goodbye, or at least a 'thanks for the hospitality.'"

"Where do you think she got the money?" Delilah knew she was on to something.

"I figured she had either come into some unexpected money, or she had a sugar daddy. You should have seen that car. It was a Mercedes coupe; top of the line; I know my cars."

"Buying a car isn't all that difficult." Delilah knew already where the money was coming from. *Was Lillian blackmailing CC?*

"Oh, you haven't heard the best part yet, Delilah. One Friday Lillian left work and didn't even take her paycheck. I told Molly, our receptionist, that if she gave me Lillian's new address I'd drop the check off at her apartment. I was sure she could use the money over the weekend. Well… you should have seen where she was living."

"Pretty bad I imagine," Delilah said her list of suspects growing larger.

"Oh, no," Lauren said throwing her hands up in the air, "Miss Thing was living in a swank apartment building. The doorman at the front desk said Miss Barrett had gone out for the evening/would I like to leave a message. I left the envelope with him and left."

"Did you question her about it?" Delilah asked.

"Oh, yes, ma'am. You know what she told me. Listen to this. One of her friends from New York City had recently moved to Houston then was promoted to a job overseas. Since the lease was for a year they asked her to stay and take care of the place. It was all I could do not to laugh in her face. I can spot a liar from a mile away; Lillian was lying."

"Lilian was afraid of something; very afraid," Lauren said softly.

Delilah stared at Lauren's face. Lauren's bright animated face became serious. "She started coming to work looking frightened and nervous about everything. I asked her what was wrong and she would start crying and walk away."

"Was someone abusing her?" Delilah was having a queasy feeling; were the calls to CC fake; or were the calls just a way to contact CC?

"As flaky as Lillian's behavior was, she always came to work or called when she wasn't coming in. One day Lillian was a no show. I called her all day trying to reach her; her scheduled clients were coming in for their appointments and no Lillian. I decided I would go over to her apartment after work and find out what was going on. You may not know this but I was the one who found her body."

"I didn't know you were the one who found her." Delilah shuddered.

"Someone had really done a job on her. She was so beaten up I didn't recognize her. The apartment was torn apart like someone was looking for something. Discovering Lillian's body was something I will never forget. I'll also never forget that handsome detective who interviewed me; what a hottie."

"His name wasn't Jordan Marsh by any chance?" Delilah watched Lauren's face light up again.

"Yeah, you know Jordan?"

"Yes, I've met Jordan," Delilah replied as she picked up her bag and handed Lauren her empty glass.

"Well, all I can say is if he knocks on your front door at midnight let him in."

Lauren's loud hoot made Delilah smile as she left the salon now being renamed Serenity Salon and Spa. Too bad Lillian hadn't found any serenity there.

Chapter Twenty-Two

Delilah sat at an outside patio table at a fabled restaurant in Houston, named, Ouisie's Table. As she looked over her notes, she didn't see Jordan Marsh walk into the restaurant and sit down at her table.

"You summoned Ms. Morgan; what exactly do you need?" Delilah scowled when she looked up from her notes. He smiled, *this wasn't going to be fun; he had already gotten on her last nerve.*

"First of all, I didn't summons you; I asked you to meet me for lunch. You are right about one thing; I do want something I want some information."

"Oh, now I'm your personal CI. That means confidential informant." He laughed.

"Oh, trust me, any information you give me will not breach your personal moral compass; or the ethics of your beloved police department."

Jordan conceded, "Okay, what kind of information are you looking for?"

Delilah leaned across the table. "I'm sure you know that Lillian Barrett's name was actually Lillian Stewart." He didn't answer. "She came to Houston from New York City. Apparently, she was a top-notch hairstylist in New York with a client list of the rich and famous. If she was gaining quite a reputation with many well-known celebrities, why move to Houston; why not Los Angeles, Miami, or Atlanta? Lillian moved to Houston because she already knew someone here. She didn't move to Houston because she knew CC. CC was well known in Houston, but she only had a few close friends who knew her in New York; she didn't have a following there." Jordan still didn't answer but smiled at her enthusiasm.

Delilah was really wound up now. "That means she had a connection here in Houston that led her to CC. My guess is it had something to do with her children, Preston and Shelby. If we can make a connection, we might be able to find out what actually happened to CC."

Jordan reached across the table and took her hand. "Delilah, you have a lot of theories, but you don't have any evidence or proof; your hands, and mine, are tied. I've personally looked into the information you gave me and I found absolutely nothing. I promise you I will continue to look into this case, but right now we have absolutely nothing concrete to go on.

"Other than her radio calls to CC; which are well known, we haven't been able to establish any other connection to the victim. Her apartment, her new car, they were apparently cash transactions in her own name. Her cell phone records don't show she called CC at the radio station or at home. The only calls she made on the phone were to her clients and a co-worker, Lauren Holloway."

Delilah thought for a moment, "Maybe Lillian and CC used burner phones to contact each other. Burner phones, as they are called, are bought at a convenience store, and are virtually untraceable; they can be thrown away after use."

"I know what a burner phone is Delilah. What I can tell you, and really shouldn't, is that Lillian Stewart left New York after the death of her husband. Perhaps she moved to Houston to drop off the radar; someplace where she wasn't known, to start over. I'm sure you'll find out her real reason for moving to Houston; being a full-fledged detective, this shouldn't be a problem for you."

To Delilah's horror, her face turned blood red. Why had she called him; he always made her feel like the village idiot. She hurriedly got up and picked up her handbag. She turned to him and said, "Jordan Marsh, has anyone ever told you you're a pompous ass?"

Jordan shrugged and raised his hand in the air. "I apologize, Delilah, sit down and let's have lunch."

As she started to walk past him, he said, "I thought we were going to have a nice, leisurely lunch and I was going to ask you out to dinner so we could get to know each other better. Now I know you only wanted information on the Barrett case."

He laughed. "I feel so used; but I would still like to have dinner with you."

Delilah leaned down to whisper in his ear, "I would rather starve to death in a third world prison than sit down and have a meal with you."

Jordan's laughter followed her as she stormed out of the restaurant, not noticing Shelby and Preston sitting at a corner table inside the restaurant.

Chapter Twenty-Three

Delilah walked into Jerry's office unannounced, sat down in a chair in front of his desk, and pushed an envelope toward him across the desk. Jerry turned from his computer and smiled.

"If it isn't my little superstar." When Delilah didn't respond, he hurried on. "What you have done for this station is unbelievable. That little venture into helping senior citizens has exploded. Your first little venture, the little salon you recommended for Tuesday specials has doubled their business. They are not only expanding they are advertising on our station. Plus, it seems every business in the city that has goods or services for senior citizens is advertising on our station. Advertising dollars and listeners are going thru the roof and I owe it all to you. What's your next venture?"

Delilah still didn't respond. Instead she leaned forward and pushed the envelope closer to him.

"What's this a demand for a raise?" He quickly opened the envelope, read the contents, then threw the letter down on his desk.

"You're kidding of course."

"No, Jerry, I'm dead serious."

"You're quitting? Why?"

Delilah kept her voice and face expressionless. "I was never cut out for this business. I was just trying to carry on for CC's listeners. This radio show was never meant to be my career choice; my life's work."

Jerry's face was slowly turning bright red. He tore up the letter and leaned across the desk.

"Let me remind you that you signed a contract with the station that is binding. If you break that contract, I will sue you for everything you have or ever hope to have." He leaned back in his chair. "If you leave, you may as well pack your bags and get out of town because I will personally see that you never work again in this city. Whether you believe me or not, try leaving KLS and I will make your life a living hell."

"Is that how you controlled CC?" Delilah shouted.

"Oh, here we go again. CC, CC, CC. When will you get it through your head that CC is gone? Her death was an accident; LET IT GO!"

"That's just it, Jerry, it wasn't an accident. CC was murdered."

"Murdered, are you out of your mind? Murdered by whom?" Jerry shouted.

"I don't know who killed her but I intend to find out."

Jerry again leaned across the desk and looked at her. "How did you come up with the conclusion that she was murdered?"

"I was at her house the night she was murdered," Delilah countered.

"What are you talking about? You need to explain yourself," Jerry was shouting at the top of his lungs and his face was alarmingly bright red.

"The night CC was killed, I broke into her house. She was being kept in deplorable conditions in one of the bedrooms in the house. Someone had tied her to the bed and basically forgotten she existed. There is no way she could have gotten in a wheelchair, wheeled herself down to the pool, and committed what appeared to be suicide; it's just not possible."

"Did you talk to her?" Jerry asked anxiously.

"She was so traumatized and confused she couldn't speak. I went to get help for her, but I was too late. I think that view of her in that condition will be with me for the rest of my life." Delilah could feel the tears beginning in her eyes and quickly wiped them away. Tears to Jerry was a sign of weakness.

Jerry smiled, "Simple explanation, Delilah. The house has an elevator, CC could have easily wheeled herself into the elevator, gone done to the first floor, and wheeled herself out to the pool."

Delilah looked at him in astonishment. "I'm telling you she was in no condition to wheel herself anywhere. Her children were home; they were arguing as usual. The house alarm would have gone off when she opened the door to go outside; they would have heard the alarm."

Jerry was now openly laughing, "So now her children killed her; is that what you're saying?"

Delilah stood up and picked up her bag. "No, what I'm saying is that CC did not commit suicide, she was murdered and that murder was connected in some way with the murder of Lillian Barrett."

Jerry continued laughing, "Well, Nancy Drew, continue on with your investigation, but you have a show to do today."

He turned back to his computer. "Oh, by the way, the next time you come to see me, make an appointment like the rest of the staff."

As Delilah walked out into the lobby, Norma informed her, "Your voice mail is full, I took these messages for you."

Norma looked at the expression on her face and asked, "How did it go?"

Delilah replied, "It didn't."

Norma pushed an envelope across the desk. The envelope looked as if it had been soaked in water then dried. Norma winked at Delilah, "The police gave Elizabeth's personal effects to her brother and CC's letter was in her purse: maybe her letter will brighten your day."

"I should have done more to save her life," Delilah said sadly.

Norma shook her head. "It was not your fault Delilah; keep in mind, all her old staff was fired, there was no one to hear her cries for help."

Chapter Twenty-Four

Delilah sat in her office with the envelope Norma had given her held tightly in her hand. Norma sat across the desk from her eagerly waiting for her to read the letter. The letter showed definite signs of having been soaked in water. Delilah carefully slit the envelope open thinking that it would be unreadable if it was written in ink; to her surprise, the letter was carefully typed. Clearing her throat Delilah began reading out loud.

Dear Delilah,

I know this letter to you will come as a complete surprise, but as my health and current situation deteriorates every passing day, it is time for me to finally clear the decks with both you and Norma. Both of you have always supported me and given me unconditional loyalty; for this, I say thank you and God Bless you. I have been difficult and unkind to you both for years and I hope you will someday forgive me.

You have tremendous talent, Delilah. I recognized it and was sometimes jealous of your talent. Being selfish and self-centered instead of encouraging you I tried my best to hold you back. I knew the first day I heard you on the radio, sitting in for me, that my time as a radio personality was coming to an end. I spouted off to anyone who would listen, mainly my children, how you had stolen all the things I had worked for over the years. They believed me and they tried to mount a campaign against you, but it didn't work; no one believed them. It was too late to make amends for some of the lives I destroyed; I've made too many enemies. I immediately recognized your talent; that talent I kept under wraps for many years. Keep up the good work, Delilah; it is your time to shine.

Enough of this maudlin tone, there are things I need to tell you. Elizabeth has, on two occasions when my children were not in the house, brought in my lawyer Mason Evans to make some changes to my will. The changes have been made, notarized, and filed so my wishes will be granted.

It is getting late and my children will be returning soon, I don't want to put Elizabeth in jeopardy. I still have so much to tell you; I will try to communicate with you again. Thank you again for all you have done for me; It is too bad that I realized too late what an important part you both you and Norma played in my life. I would sign this letter Love CC, but you already know my friends what you have meant to me.

CC

Tears flowed freely from both Delilah and Norma. Delilah folded the letter and put it back in the envelope. She stood up leaning heavily on the table. Looking down at Norma's bowed head she said tearfully, "If it's the last thing I do, I'm going to find out who murdered CC."

Norma looked up at her, wiping her eyes, "You can count on me to help you, Delilah, I'll do whatever it takes to find out what really happened to CC."

Chapter Twenty-Five

Delilah and Norma sat in a car across the street from the River Oaks Loft Apartments. Norma looked across the street and whistled under her breath. "Girlfriend was living large for a hairstylist with no clients."

"Exactly," Delilah said rolling down the car window. "CC was bankrolling her and I'm going to find out why. Do you remember your instructions before I go in?"

"Of course, I remember," Norma replied, "I watch Criminal Minds every week. You, Delilah Morgan, are about to become a criminal if this plan fails."

Delilah got out of the car, crossed the street, and walked into the posh apartment building. The young woman at the front desk looked Delilah up and down with a smile that hinted that perhaps she might have come in the building by mistake. From the woman's look, Delilah knew she would have to do her best CC imitation.

"Hello, I'm Delilah Morgan from KLS Radio." She handed the woman a business card. "I understand you have some units for lease. My realtor is so hair-brained, I think she's taken me to every dump in town, so I decided to take matters into my own hands."

"What do you have available?"

"Let me first say, Ms. Morgan, that I live with my mother and grandmother and they absolutely swear by your show…"

"What do you have available?" Delilah cut her off sharply the way CC had done to her on many occasions. She hoped her no-nonsense approach would work.

The young lady stood up from behind the desk. "We do have two units on the fourth floor but only one is available at the moment."

Bingo. Delilah thought. Lillian lived on the fourth floor.

"Why can't I see both units?" Delilah demanded.

The young woman's face turned red. "One unit is completely empty, the other is undergoing…" She paused for a moment searching for the right words. "The other unit is uh… undergoing some renovations." She reached into the desk and brought out a small keyring.

Renovation after a murder you mean, Delilah thought silently.

"Very well, let's see the units," Delilah said in the haughty voice. Delilah punched a number into her cell phone, and at the same instant, the telephone on the desk rang.

The young girl answered the telephone, listened for a moment, then quickly turned to Delilah; a distressed look on her face, "I'm sorry, Ms. Morgan, but I have to handle this call."

"Give me the keys, I'll take a quick look and come right back." Delilah smiled and held out her hand.

"I can't do that, Ms. Morgan, I could lose my job if I give you these keys. Our building manager is the only one allowed to show the units."

"You'll lose more than your job if I let it be known how I was treated when I came to this rather dubious address; Keep in mind my opinion carries a lot of influence in this town; now give me the keys and finish your little business on the telephone." Delilah snatched the keys out of her hand and marched to the elevator as if she, at the moment, was visiting royalty. On the elevator, Delilah felt guilty about how she had treated the young girl. She knew exactly how it felt to be bullied and threatened; to be left not knowing if you had said or done the wrong thing that could mean you could lose your job.

Delilah slipped into the first empty apartment, closed the door, and put on the latex gloves Norma had given her. She could still hear Norma's instructions. "Put on the gloves so there is no DNA and be quick, and fast. I don't know how long I will be able to keep this woman on the telephone."

Delilah quickly looked in her CC's address book. Lillian telephone number, address, and apartment number were listed under LB. Hopefully, the apartment number was right. Slipping out of the empty apartment, she walked down the empty corridor and found Apartment 412. She put the key in the lock and slipped inside.

Undergoing renovations was an understatement. There was black powder on every visible surface. Delilah stepped carefully over some items that had been knocked over and went over to her desk. The police had probably taken her computer and cell phone; all the desk drawers were empty; no papers or notes were anywhere in sight, only office supplies.

The bedroom was an even bigger mess. The mattress on the bed was turned sideways, all the bureau drawers were empty, and there was a huge stain on the floor next to the bed. Delilah opened the door to a huge walk-in closet and gasped. The closet was filled from floor to ceiling with racks of clothes and shoes. How in the world, did a hairstylist, with no real clients afford all these things? Looking at the labels on some of the garments they were from some of the high-class designers' CC had favored. When she picked up a red bottom shoe from the shoe rack to examine it, a small key fell from the shoe. As she picked up the key, her cell phone rang. Norma uttered only one word, "Incoming."

Delilah dropped the shoe and quickly left the apartment. As she walked down the long hall, peeling off the gloves and sticking them in her pocket, the Building Manager got off the elevator.

The woman was in a complete panic. "I think you were looking at the wrong apartment, Ms. Morgan."

"No, I wasn't." Delilah lied. "I was simply checking to see how many apartments were on this floor, security cameras, fire exits, that type of thing. I would have asked you about them if you hadn't been so BUSY."

"I'm sorry, I could have sworn I saw you on camera going into the other empty apartment." She said sheepishly. "How did you know the other apartment was empty?"

"How did I know about the other unit, your receptionist told me." Delilah gave her a laugh that was more nervous than funny.

Cameras, Delilah thought. *I forgot about the cameras. How could I be so stupid? Now they had me on tape.*

"Yes, we had cameras installed a few weeks ago after…" She didn't finish her sentence.

Delilah quickly changed the subject, "I saw all the black dirt on the door of the apartment down the hall and I hoped I wouldn't be moving into an apartment with filthy neighbors. That's either here or there; here are your keys. I'll let you know what I decide about the empty apartments. For the amount of entertaining I do, that first apartment seemed rather small. The apartment undergoing renovations is much larger; it would meet my needs much better."

Delilah stepped on the elevator and before the Building Manager, could lock the apartment door and follow her, Delilah pushed the button on the inside of the elevator, and the doors closed.

Delilah left the building and hurried across the street to the KLS company car. Norma was sitting behind the wheel. Delilah looked through the window which was halfway down.

"Why are you in the driver's seat?"

Norma lowered her sunglasses and stared at her, "Get in the back seat, Sherlock Holmes, no one as bourgeois as you're pretending to be would drive themselves around town." Delilah was barely in the back seat before Norma pulled away from the curb.

Chapter Twenty-Six

Delilah caught up with Norma as she left the office for the day. "Did you have any luck with the key?"

Norma dug into her hand bag and handed Delilah the key. "This key is for a storage locker."

"Oh, that helps a lot. There must be thousands of storage units in Houston. We may never find the right one."

Norma looked at her over the top of her glasses. "If you had a storage unit, where would it be?"

Delilah thought for a moment. "It would be near where I lived, in case I wanted to pick up something."

"Bingo," Norma replied. "I called her apartment building and told the receptionist that I was picking up Lillian's furniture tomorrow but there was no information on the order about where it was to be delivered. She told me Ace Moving and Storage was near their building and the apartment building' used them for excess storage. I called Ace Storage and told them I had noticed a leak in my storage unit and could they check it out. I gave them Lillian's name and key number. Guess what? Lillian has a unit there."

Delilah stepped forward to give her a hug but Norma stepped back out of her reach.

"Look, Delilah," Norma said, handing her the key and a piece of paper, "Jerry really read me the riot act today, he thinks you are delusional and he doesn't want me to help you in any way in pursuing what he calls a wild goose chase trying to prove CC was murdered. He threatened me with many things, like loss of employment. I'll keep helping you, but at the station, you and I cannot be seen pursuing this project. What we do on our own time is none of his business."

"I'm sorry I put you in this position, Norma. I don't want you to lose your job."

Norma laughed, "Girl if I had a dollar every time Jerry threatened to fire me, I would have enough money to retire years ago. I know where all the bones are buried at KLS, but I also don't want to end up like Lillian Barrett or CC. I do love my job, but with Jerry's new-found money, and his grand plans for KLS it may be out with the old, meaning me, and in with the new."

"Do you think Jerry has anything to do with the murders?"

Norma laughed out loud. "Jerry Wainwright, are you kidding me? He may be many things, but he's not a murderer; he wouldn't dirty his hands with murder. What Jerry would do is make your life so miserable you'd wish you were dead."

"Tomorrow is Saturday. I'll go to the storage unit and check it out. Trust me, Norma, I will keep your involvement in this mess to a minimum."

"Oh, no, you don't," Norma said, "I'm just going undercover; I'm still in. Maybe we should buy burner telephones to keep in touch." Norma walked away shaking her head, *Solving a murder calls for being very, very careful; I read that tip in my last murder mystery book.*

Chapter Twenty-Seven

Delilah was surprised that on a Saturday morning, Ace Moving and Storage was completely deserted. The gate to the facility was open, the small office had its blinds drawn and no one responded when she knocked on the office door. Not knowing if going on this search alone was a good idea or a bad idea she started walking through the facility looking for Lillian storage unit.

Storage unit number '5' was located at the back of the facility next to a weed-choked lot filled with not only weeds but apparently a dumping ground for abandoned items. It took a few minutes to find the unit but with the key, it was easy to open the locked door. She stepped inside the unit and flipped on a light switch containing a bulb that must have been 40 watts; it was very dim. Most of the light came in thru the open door.

To her surprise, the small unit was completely empty with the exception of a small file cabinet pushed into the corner. *Thank goodness, Norma hadn't come with her. She would be cursing at the top of her lungs.*

Delilah quickly started opening the file drawers. She opened the top drawer, empty; the second drawer was also empty; empty if you didn't count the bugs that had met their demise scattered in the corners of the drawers. Opening the third drawer, she found a yellow, manila envelope and a small binder. As she quickly put the items into her large canvas bag, the lights went out and she heard the padlock click on the door. She ran in the darkness to the door but it was locked and despite all her pushing it would not budge.

Finding her cellphone in her bag, she turned on the small light on the phone. *Think, think*, she said to herself; *don't panic. I'll call; who I should call; not the police, they would question why she was there in the first place. Norma; no, she couldn't break the padlock. I'll call Jordan; surely he would come and rescue her; or maybe not.*

Praying for a signal on her phone, she saw the contact number she had reluctantly let him put in her phone and quickly punched in his number.

"Hello," he answered. as if he had been in a deep sleep and didn't want to talk.

"Jordan, it's Delilah, I need your help."

"Delilah who?" he said in a joking manner, now he was fully awake.

"Delilah Morgan, you know who I am. I need your help, someone locked me in a storage unit and I can't get out."

She could tell he was enjoying her dilemma, he was almost laughing on the phone. "Have you called 911?" He was really enjoying himself.

"No, I made an error in judgment and called you."

He loved it when she was annoyed and was on the verge of screaming. "Where are you?"

"I'm at Ace Moving and Storage on 15th Street, Unit 5. Please hurry. How long will it take you to get here?"

"If I come in my underwear and rev up my helicopter, I should be there in about five minutes." He waited for a smart come back from Delilah; he didn't hear one.

He could hear the panic in her voice. He said in a reassuring voice, "Traffic will be light this early in the morning so I should be there in about twenty minutes."

"Can't you put on those flashing lights and get here quicker?"

"If you wanted all that fanfare, you should have called 911." Before she could reply he hung up the phone.

****

Leaning back in his chair in Delilah's small kitchen, Jordan only said one word, "Explain."

"What's to explain," Delilah said, placing a cup of coffee in front of him on the kitchen table. "You know as well as I do that CC did not commit suicide."

"I know that because…"

"I was at the house the night CC died. She was in no condition to get in a wheelchair, get down to the main floor, then wheel herself out to the swimming pool. She couldn't have done it alone."

"So, you're saying someone put her on the elevator, wheeled her outside, and pushed her into the pool? Why would someone do that, they already had her locked away. You said they wouldn't let anyone see or talk to her. Why didn't they just let her die naturally?"

"Did they do an autopsy? What did they find?"

"You know very well I can't discuss the autopsy results with you, and please, please don't think about breaking into the Medical Examiner's office; break-ins seem to be your specialty these days."

Delilah could feel her face slowly turning red; she could barely contain her anger. "What are you talking about?"

"First of all, you went to Lillian Barrett's apartment; not a good idea. Next not being a first-rate detective, instead of giving them an alias, you give them a business card. Next, regardless of the fact that almost every building has security cameras, they watched you go down to Lillian's apartment and go inside. However, I must congratulate you on the latex gloves, which was a nice touch."

"Get out of my house," Delilah screamed. Everything he said was true and it galled her that she hadn't thought of any of this.

"I know you're upset, Delilah, about CC death, and I promise you I will help any way I can; but let ME do it. Believe me, I am on your side; stop trying to do this alone."

"I do feel like I'm alone in this. No one, not even you, believe me, but I promise you I won't do anything else without letting you know."

"Did you find anything we missed while you were in her apartment?"

Yes, the key to her storage unit in a shoe, Delilah thought silently.

"You said you didn't find anything in the storage unit but an empty file cabinet." He gave her a questioning look.

Delilah felt the canvas bag with the manila envelope and the notebook rub up against her leg under the table. She smiled at Jordan, "Didn't find a thing. Another dead end."

Chapter Twenty-Eight

Delilah sat at her small kitchen table with Lillian's notebook and manila envelope laid out in front of her. As she fingered the two items, she silently wondered if she should have shared this information with Jordan; sometimes two heads were better than one; no, she had made the right decision. Jordan would have taken the information, he had a perfect right, after all, he was the police. If she was taken out of the loop and given no further information; she would wonder forever what had really happened to CC.

She opened the black notebook and thumbed through it. Items you would normally have on your computer were carefully written in the notebook; client names, addresses, appointments, passwords; all were carefully recorded. Delilah was startled when she read the last page of the notebook. There were four names listed:

Shelby Clark
Preston Clark
Cassandra Clark
Jerry Wainwright

What was the connection between these four people? She knew about CC's connection to Lillian, but Shelby, Preston, and Jerry. How did this all fit together?

Delilah dumped the contents of the manila folder on the table. The folder contained only a newspaper article.

Death of Nathan Barrett, son of billionaire Michael Barrett shakes the banking world.

Nathan Barrett, 37, son of billionaire Michael Barrett, accidentally plunged to his death on June 14 after an altercation with his wife and friends following a dinner party. Police sources say Nathan and his wife were arguing on the balcony of their Park Avenue apartment when the argument became physical. Their dinner guests, Shelby and Preston Clark attempted to separate them. During the altercation, Mr. Barret accidentally fell over the railing. The NYPD, in the past few days, has ruled out homicide and have dropped charges against both Mrs. Barrett and the Clarkes. Nathan Barrett's funeral is scheduled for June 15 at 2:00 PM at St Joseph's Chapel.

Delilah sat for a moment then reached for her cell phone and dialed Jordan's number. She didn't wait for him to acknowledge her call.

"Jordan, I need to apologize to you. I didn't tell you the whole story."

"I know," was his only reply.

"How do you know?" She could feel her anger starting to build.

"You forget I'm a trained detective, I have been trained to see beyond the obvious. You have one of those honest faces that send out signals when you're not telling the truth. I admire your honest face and your enthusiasm to get to the truth. What you need to improve upon are your detective skills." She thought she heard him laughing.

"What didn't you tell me?"

"The file cabinet in Lillian's storage unit wasn't empty?"

"WHAT!" he shouted. "What did you find?"

"I found a notebook and a newspaper clipping."

"And you thought it was not necessary to share this information with the investigating detective? I could have you arrested for withholding information."

"I need you to come back to my house; I want to share this information with you." Delilah thought for a minute. "I know you have to drive all the way back across town to my house, but I can assure you it will be well worth your time." She waited.

"I don't have to drive across town; I parked down the street from your house."

"Why are you parked on my street?"

"When I first came to your house there was a car parked across the street from your house with someone crouched down in the seat. What caught my attention was there were no license plates on the car. I drove around the block, parked my car, and watched your house from a distance."

"Are they still out there?" Delilah said nervously.

"No, they just drove away. Close your blinds; I'm on my way. I have to hurry in case he plays the same trick on me and circles the block."

"Am I in danger?" Delilah asked as she pulled Jordan thru her front door.

"Well, somebody locked you in that storage unit, and someone is definitely watching your house. I'd say someone is interested in what you are doing. You need to be careful; start by closing your blinds at least at night. I sat in my car and watched you through your window moving around the house; that is not a good thing."

"I'll take that into consideration," Delilah said thrusting the newspaper article into his hands, "Read this."

Jordan sat down and read the article. He handed it back to Delilah. "And."

"That's the connection I was looking for between CC and Lillian Barrett."

"What's the connection? Jordan asked slowly. Was he finally beginning to believe CC was murdered?"

"She was blackmailing CC."

"So, you think CC killed her."

"No, of course not; maybe Lillian was blackmailing CC. You didn't know CC; she was a very prideful woman. CC would rip your life apart on radio and in her newspaper column, but she never ever wanted a breath of scandal about her or her family. Her career was slowly slipping away from her and she knew a scandal, any scandal, would push her over the edge. CC's so-called friends and associates tolerated her, but they didn't like her; they merely tolerated her because of Robert and the cache he held in the community. She would have paid any amount of money to keep up that front; even pay blackmail."

"If Lillian was blackmailing CC about the incident in New York with her children, CC must have known they all had been cleared and it had been ruled an accidental death."

Delilah thought for a moment, "She must have known something else CC wanted covered up. When we find out what CC wanted kept hidden, we will find CC and Lillian's killer."

"WE?" Jordan said. He got up walked to the window and looked through the blinds to be sure they weren't being watched. There were cars on the street but they all appeared empty.

"I think I'll sleep on your couch tonight," Jordan said casually.

"Why?" Delilah said.

"Since you have chosen to go rogue, you need backup; who better to fill that role than a *real* cop? I don't know whether the person following you is a danger to you or whether you're a bigger danger to yourself."

Chapter Twenty-Nine

Shelby Clarke sat in the small interrogation room at the Houston Police Department and checked her makeup in the small make up mirror she kept in her purse. A small smile was reflected in the mirror; a sly but knowing smile. Jordan Marsh had at last called her. She had met him recently at a dinner party he and his aunt had attended. Shelby had pulled him into a conversation after dinner and he had reluctantly taken her phone number. She knew he would call; they always did. Men loved to play the 'I'm not interested games'; but they always called. Jordan was handsome, unmarried, and rich; those were her top three requirements for any man she pursued.

Jordan walked into the interrogation room carrying a manila folder and sat down across the table from her.

"Thank you for coming down to the station, Ms. Clark—"

Shelby interrupted him, "After all these years you call me Ms. Clark; remember we do have a history." She leaned forward giving him a bird's eye view of her cleavage.

"Shelby," he said, ignoring her attempt to throw him off track. "You might not know this, but I'm the lead detective on your mother's death, and I'm trying to tie up some loose ends."

"You called me down here regarding my mother's death?" She started to stand up.

"My mother committed suicide; what else could there be to 'tie up'?" She sounded annoyed, as she suddenly realized he had no real interest in her; he was in fact trying to get information.

"What loose ends?"

Jordan cut to the chase. "Did you know Lillian Barrett?"

"Lillian Barrett, the name sounds familiar; let me think for a minute." She looked around the room as if to dredge up the memory of the woman.

"Oh, yes," she said sweetly. "I believe she was a friend of my mother's."

"A friend of your mother's but not yours?"

"No, not a friend of mine. I have very few female friends, I prefer male company." She gave him a dazzling smile and again leaned forward flaunting her cleavage.

Jordan again ignored her. He pushed the newspaper article across the table and she picked it up and read it.

When she looked up the smile had disappeared, she was ghastly pale but she quickly regained her composure. "Oh, that Lillian Barrett, yes, Preston and I met her in New York. You know how you briefly meet someone and you forget their name?"

"An accidental death and you completely forget about it? What really happened in New York, Shelby? I want the truth."

Seeing the look on his face Shelby swallowed and then started her story. "I met Lillian in New York on a fashion shoot. She knew a lot of celebrities and had a lot of upscale clients. She said she would make sure I got into their circle; the sky would be the limit. Yes, we became casual friends; then everything changed. One day at lunch she confided in me that she wanted to get out of her marriage, but she had signed a prenup, and it was going to be difficult to get around it. His family was wealthy and at all costs, they would pay her off to avoid scandal; she had a fool-proof plan. If her plan worked, she would split her good fortune with Preston and me and we would never have to worry about money again. I didn't know what she had planned, but she invited Preston and me to dinner the next weekend. During the dinner, she told her husband that she wanted a divorce. She went on to say that she and I had become lovers and she no longer wanted to be married to him. That was all a complete lie.

"I was shocked that she had involved me that way," Shelby said tearfully. "Lillian outlined her monetary demands to him and told him what she would do to him and his family's good name if he didn't go along with her demands. Her husband was furious; he called us every name you could think of, then went out on the balcony to have a smoke. Lillian ran outside after him, pleading with him to let her go; he turned around and struck her with his fist. Preston and I ran out on the balcony to stop his assault and in our struggle, he grabbed me around the neck and started choking me; he was choking me so hard I almost lost consciousness. Preston managed to get him off of me and the three of us tried to get him under control, but he struggled so hard that in the struggle he fell over the edge of the balcony; it was an accident. After the police saw

Lillian's face and the bruises on my neck we were eventually cleared of all charges, but she wouldn't let it go." Shelby was close to tears.

"Only she followed you to Houston and started blackmailing you and then your mother," Jordan added.

"That sniveling coward called me several times crying on the phone. She said her husband's father owned the apartment she and her husband had lived in and had promptly kicked her out of the building. Somehow the owner of the salon where she worked didn't like the notoriety her presence in the salon created and asked her to leave. She had managed to find another salon, but it wasn't in a location her clients wanted to be seen in so she lost most of her clientele. The last time she called she said all she had left was the few pieces of jewelry her husband had given her; when she pawned the jewelry and that money ran out, she would be out on the street. I told her it was her own fault and hung up on her."

"Apparently she bought a ticket to Houston and started a blackmail scheme on you and your brother; so, you killed her."

Shelby jumped up; turning over her chair in the process. "I didn't kill her; why would I? When she saw how Preston and I lived under our mother's thumb and had no money, she was through with us; my mother was another story. My mother wined and dined her until it made me sick. I could have cared less if she told anyone about what happened in New York; we had been cleared of all charges. She must have had something else on my mother because my mother continued paying her until the day my father died; then she stopped."

"So there's a possibility your mother killed her or had someone kill her?" Jordan asked.

"My mother didn't kill her. They became friends; really good friends. They went to lunch and dinner together constantly; they even went on several trips together. The only difference in my mother, that I noticed, was that she was beginning to drink more and more. She told me once when I asked her about Lillian, she told me not to worry about Lillian, everything was being taken care of; I never asked her what she meant; then Lillian turned up dead."

"How did she react after Lillian died?" Jordan had her on a roll. He was getting valuable information.

"She literally fell apart. Her drinking was getting worst. I confided in Jerry and he thought it best if we kept her under wraps for a while."

"Under wraps? What does that mean?" Jordan was writing in his notebook.

"We would keep her out of the public eye; get her some alcohol counseling and start encouraging her to make a comeback."

"What about your brother; was he involved in your plan?"

"What about my brother?" Shelby sneered. "Give him an unlimited supply of drugs and alcohol and he could care less what goes on in the world. Since my mother's death, he seldom leaves the house; if he does leave, it's only to get more drugs. Preston murdering someone; that's a joke. He doesn't have the gumption to get out of bed some days."

Shelby got up again and went to the door and opened it. "If I'm not under arrest, I'm leaving. Enjoyed our little chat."

Before she left, she looked over her shoulder. "If you need any more information, call our family's lawyer; if you want to reach me personally," she winked and smiled, "you have my number."

Chapter Thirty

Delilah opened the door to her office and paused in the doorway. If she worked at KLS forever, this would never really feel like her office; this was, and would always be CC's office. CC's private domain, her throne room. Shelby and Preston had done a good job of clearing out the office. There were faded outlines on the wall where CC had hung her very expensive paintings. Her photos taken with every celebrity she could manage to take a photo with were missing. Delilah always wondered why there were never any pictures of her family or her children; it was as if they didn't exist. CC demanded that flowers fill her office every day without fail. Sometimes there were so many flowers the room resembled a funeral home and put Delilah's allergies on red alert. When she asked CC about the flowers, her only reply was, "As hard as I work, flowers are the least KLS can do for me."

She sat down in the rickety desk chair Norma had rescued from the storeroom. The ergonomic chair CC had demanded had disappeared along with her computer, printer, and copier. They had taken everything. Delilah silently wondered; *didn't anything belong to the station.*

The only thing that belonged to Delilah now was the rickety desk chair and the aloe vera plant that was on the window sill. Delilah would ask Norma to get her computer and printer out of her old cubicle and have it installed in her new office; it was old but would beat no office equipment at all.

There were two telephones on the desk, one for use within the office; the other one, which was bright red, was CC's personal phone. The red phone was the one CC used the most. How many rumors and gossip she received on that phone would never be known. Delilah didn't know what the phone number was; she doubted anyone knew the number; CC at times was very, very secretive.

As she pulled the red phone across the desk, to her surprise, it started ringing.

"Well, hello, Delilah Morgan, remember me?"

"Who are you?" Delilah asked. "Your voice sounds familiar."

"I'm disappointed you don't recognize me. It's me, Lillian Barrett, Lilly B, LB." There was laughter on the other end of the line.

"Is this some kind of joke?" Delilah asked. "Lillian Barrett is dead."

"No, my dear I am very much alive." Again there was laughter on the line.

Delilah countered, "They found your body; someone had beaten you so badly…"

"They found a body but it wasn't mine." The voice sounded amused.

"If it wasn't you, then who was it?" Delilah tried to keep the caller talking.

"That body they found was a friend of mine who came down from New York and decided to try to continue the scam I had just finished with CC. She thought she could squeeze out a few more dollars; it ended up costing her her life."

"Lillian, you've got to go to the police. You need to tell them what happened and clear your name. If you didn't have anything to do with CC's death, there is nothing they can do to you."

"Are you crazy?" The voice sounded amused at Delilah's suggestion "I got just what I came for, revenge and money, and as soon as I got what I wanted, I was through with the Clark clan; may they all rot in hell."

"What about CC; she was your friend." Delilah knew she was sounding as if she was begging.

"CC was a dupe. It was her own fault, she was so easy to blackmail. It started with her trying to cover up what happened in New York, then after a few drinks, she began telling me her deepest and darkest secrets which made my cash payoff grow bigger and bigger. If she hadn't had so much pride; so afraid of losing her social standing and reputation, she would have told me to go to hell. Instead, she decided to pay me; blackmail money was her only solution. CC had one secret she never, ever wanted revealed. If that particular information was revealed, her husband and all the people in her life that she had gossiped and threatened with scandal would descend on her and ruin her life."

"What was her secret?" Delilah asked.

"Are you really that naïve, Delilah? If I tell you all CC's secrets, your life won't be worth a plug nickel."

"What about your life?" Delilah demanded.

"The minute I got the last of my pay off, I put the lights of Houston, Texas in my rear-view mirror. I'm someplace now where no one will ever find me. They'll discover soon enough that the body they found is not me, but by that time I'll be so far away the killer will never find me."

"So you know who killed CC and your friend?" Delilah demanded. The answer to her question was a dial tone.

Chapter Thirty-One

Delilah rushed through the radio station lobby, completely ignoring Norma who was waving an envelope at her. Norma gave her a puzzled look when Delilah turned around and shouted, "She's alive. She's alive."

Delilah burst through the door to Jerry's office, completely ignoring his steadfast rules; call before you come to my office, and never come in unannounced. Delilah sat down in front of Jerry's desk and repeated her hurried message. "She's alive. She's alive."

Jerry looked up from the papers he was reading and stared at Delilah. He gave her the look you gave a naughty child before you disciplined them. "Who's alive, Delilah?"

"Lillian Barrett is alive." When he gave her a puzzled look, Delilah went on.

"Don't you see I'm off the hook; I was not responsible in any way for Lillian Barret's death; I had nothing to do with it."

Jerry leaned across the desk and stared at her. "Delilah, I'm beginning to be seriously worried about you." When Delilah started to speak, he held up his hand.

"One day you come rushing in saying, this Lillian person is dead. Today you come in here saying she's alive. What leads you to believe she's alive?"

"I just spoke with her on the phone?"

Jerry leaned back in his chair and gave her an incredulous look. "If you just talked to her on the phone Delilah, it was probably a prank call. Someone is playing a joke on you; Lillian Barrett is dead."

"No, Jerry, the person who called me had information a prankster would not have known." It was her turn to hold up her hand to stop Jerry from answering. "She knew about what happened in New York and how it had been covered up. She knew about blackmailing CC and how she had befriended CC to the point where CC considered her a friend. In one of CC's drunken stupors, she told Lillian all of her well-kept secrets."

"This person knew all of this?" Jerry asked.

"You haven't heard the best part yet. One of Lillian's friends from New York came to Houston to visit Lillian. Apparently, Lillian had gotten her last payoff from CC and was on her way out of town, but the friend decided to stick around to keep the scam going a little longer; that error in judgment cost her friend her life."

"Thank goodness, this drama is finally over; its back to business as usual." Jerry turned around and proceeded to type on his computer.

Delilah got out of her chair and walked to the door. "Oh, it's not over by a long shot," she announced. "I'm going to find out who murdered CC and why; then it will be over." She looked back at Jerry as she walked out of his office; he sat in stunned silence.

Norma stopped Delilah as she walked across the lobby and thrust an envelope into her hand.

"I've been trying to get your attention all morning. Open the envelope; if it's the same as the one delivered to me, we are both supposed to go to the reading of CC's will on Friday."

"Why would CC want us to go to the reading of her will? It seems to me that her will would involve family members only; not us."

"Well, you can stay at home if you want to," Norma informed her. "As for me, I'm going just to see the greedy look on her children's faces. It would make my day if she didn't leave those two ungrateful brats a dime. Remember, Robert Clarke didn't leave either one of them a dime; it would make my day if CC did the same."

"Now you've piqued my interest. I'll go with you to the reading of the will; maybe I can pick up a clue to who had the motive to murder CC."

"Let's go to dinner tonight, Norma, I have to fill you in on what happened today."

Norma raised an eyebrow, "Does this have anything to do with 'she's alive, she's alive'?"

"Never mind," Norma said shaking her head, "I'll meet you at Dexter's Place at 6:00 tonight."

Chapter Thirty-Two

Norma sat across the table at Dexter's and watched Delilah drink her second Martini She smiled when Delilah leaned across the table and shook her finger at her. "I can't imagine why we were invited to the reading of CC's will. I can see her two children, Preston and Shelby, being there; but why Jerry Wainright; and why us?"

Norma sipped her drink, "After that letter she wrote you, CC may have left you something, but me, that's really a mystery. CC and I were, what kids these days call, 'frienemies'. She knew better than to play the role of queen of the manor with me because she knew I wouldn't hesitate, job or no job, to put her in her place. We operated on the Norma Principle: You don't mess with me and I don't mess with you."

"I always wondered why she never raised her voice at you, never made unreasonable demands on you. It was like she was somehow intimidated by you. What juicy tidbits did you have on her?"

"Juicy tidbits?" Norma laughed. "Delilah Morgan, you are a strange creature from another planet. I didn't know anything about CC's personal life outside the station, but she thought I did. I did sometimes know what went on at the radio station, but she and Jerry thought I knew exactly what was truly going on at all times. I never bothered to come clean and tell them I didn't know as much as they thought. I let them think what they wanted; I could care less.

"What I *want to see tomorrow,*" Norma said laughing, "is the look on CC's children's faces if, like their father, CC didn't leave them a dime; better yet insist that they work for their money. Dole out the money to them penny by penny. If that happened, I will get up and do my Zumba dance on the table shouting, 'Hallelujah, justice has at last been served.'"

"Let's look at the cast of characters that will be there tomorrow," Delilah said taking a notepad out of her purse. "Who do you think might have wanted CC out of the way bad enough to kill her." Norma shrugged leaned over the table and snagged a hand full of peanuts.

Delilah started writing. "Well, there is Shelby whose concern for her mother at times seemed genuine. On the other hand, she also seems to be a bit callous and cold-blooded when money is involved. She will probably flip out when the two of us walk in the room." Delilah mused. "Maybe I need another Martini to sharpen my mind."

"I don't think so. Keep talking Sherlock," Norma said with a smile.

"As you wish, Watson. I don't believe Preston would hurt anyone. He walks around in an alcohol-induced haze most of the time. However, he seems to be completely under Shelby's control. We can eliminate Preston. What about Jerry?" Delilah asked.

Norma shook her head. "Jerry and CC's relationship is hard to describe. His only interest is in making sure KLS stays a viable and profitable enterprise. CC gave him cash from time to time, but I don't know what for. He still needs an influx of cash in order to keep the station running."

Delilah pushed her empty glass across the table. "I am sure one or all of them, Preston, Shelby, or Jerry, know who murdered CC. I just need more time to figure out which one. If I had my pick, I would say Shelby. The woman has no conscience."

Norma helped Delilah out of her chair. "Come on, I'll drive you home."

Delilah pulled away from Norma's firm grip. "I can drive myself home; I'm fine."

"Driving yourself home would be a neat trick since I drove us here and you didn't bring your own car. Let's go, we have a big day tomorrow."

Chapter Thirty-Three

Delilah looked around the conference table at the people who had been called into CC's attorney, Mason Evans, office for the reading of her will. Delilah silently counted the attendees and whispered to Norma who was seated next to her, "Only six people are here. What was CC up to in her last days?"

Shelby and Preston were sitting closest to CC's lawyer at the head of the table. Jerry Wainwright was also sitting near the head of the table; the seating arrangement gave both Delilah and Norma a bird's eye view of three of the participants. The only person who was out of place was Elizabeth Jones's brother, William.

What in the world was he doing here? Delilah wondered silently.

Mason Evans walked into the room, looked around, then walked to the head of the table. "Thank you all for coming in for the reading of CC's will. This won't take long as CC made changes a while ago and believe me when she made the changes she was in sound mind. All her wishes were made known and are signed, sealed, and ready to deliver." He chuckled as if he was making a joke.

"However, she was adamant that you hear her final wishes directly from her, not from a pile of papers read by me to you." Mason Evans picked up a remote control, clicked a button and a huge screen descended from the ceiling behind him. He clicked another button and the screen lit up; CC's face blazed on the screen.

Everyone at the table gasped in unison; it was CC at her finest. She was propped up in bed; her hair and makeup were flawless. It was a picture of the CC they all knew; even the sly smile that was on her lips. Everyone at the table sensed the fireworks were about to start. Delilah noticed that the triumphant smile that Shelby previously had on her face had completely disappeared; even Jerry Wainwright was beginning to squirm in his chair.

"Hello everyone; glad you all could make it today." Her voice was silky and smooth; the same voice that had enchanted her radio listeners for years. She was using her smooth west Texas accent that had made listeners draw closer to their radios to hear what she had to say.

"If you are viewing this video today, I have finally gone to meet my maker. Some of you will grieve, some of you will say, 'good riddance'; some may even say I'll miss her, though I doubt that very seriously. In order to save time and relieve dear Mason from reading through a lot of legal mishmashes, I decided to do this video to give you the salient points in my will in person." CC laughed a wicked laugh that made all of the people at the table cringe.

"Let's get the financial matters out of the way first, as my children are probably shaking in their shoes because they both remember their dear departed father didn't leave them a dime. Well, 'mommy dearest', that you called me behind my back, did a little better. To my children, Shelby and Preston, I bequeath $500,000 dollars each and the house I lived in and loved for years."

Shelby jumped up from her chair; knocking over a glass of water on the table. "Five Hundred Thousand dollars; that's all. She can't do this; we're her children. Look at her, she was not in her sound mind. We'll fight this fake will; won't we, Preston?" She jabbed Preston's shoulder and he looked up at her as if he had dozed off and hadn't heard a word of what was going on.

Mason Evans turned off the video and looked directly at Shelby. "You need to control yourself, Shelby, until you hear the rest of her requests. If you will kindly take your seat, we will continue; another outburst like that and I will have you removed from this meeting." He turned around and again clicked a button on the remote; CC's face again flooded the screen,

"The bulk of my late husband's fortune, the millions of dollars he made in his lifetime, will be equally divided between his three children, Shelby, Preston, and Amanda Clark. In case none of you knew, Robert had a daughter, Amanda, from a previous relationship. Putting all that aside, I have included her in my will as the money I was leaving behind belonged to Robert and should be shared by ALL his children. If in 12 months from today, Amanda does not come forth, Robert's money will be equally divided between Shelby and Preston." The only sound in the room was the crashing of a chair as Shelby jumped up from the table and stalked out of the room. Preston, a confused look on his face, ran out of the room after her.

"I am leaving my dear friend Elizabeth Jones's brother a \$100,000, and with what Elizabeth left him in her will from Robert's generous bequeath, he will be able to live comfortably for his remaining years. Elizabeth would have wanted that."

"Now let's get down to KLS Radio business." Jerry shifted in his chair.

"For years, Jerry Wainwright told the world about station owners and shareholders, and that the decisions he made were based on what they wanted to be done. Well, world, there were no station owners or shareholders. Jerry owned 50% of the station and Robert and I owned the other 50%. Robert never cared about KLS, he left that strictly up to me; and I failed; I failed miserably. I let Jerry take care of everything because I was too busy being a star, an icon in the community.

"As for my 50% of KLS Radio, I leave 25% to my loyal Personal Assistant, Delilah Morgan, and the other 25% to Norma Tate, both of whom faithfully helped me through years of trials and tribulations; never asking for a thing in return. I salute you both, but be wiser than I was, 'watch your back.'"

"You stupid..." Jerry yelled as he stalked from the room.

CC's voice echoed from the screen, "Jerry, this is the last time you get to call me 'stupid'." CC's loud laughter could be heard in the room as the screen went blank.

"Thank goodness, it is finally over," Mason Evans said as he gathered up his papers from the table. "If you three will follow me, I have some papers for you to sign."

Elizabeth's brother followed him out of the room; Delilah and Norma sat in stunned silence.

Chapter Thirty-Four

Shelby and Preston settled into a seat in a secluded corner of the Windsor Café an eatery across the street from Mason Evans office. A waiter immediately appeared at the table with menus and asked for their drink order. "We will both take a glass of your mango and strawberry tea," Shelby said with a warning glance at Preston.

"I really need a real drink, Shelby," Preston said with a frown.

"I want you to have a clear head while we discuss our next move. Maybe we should hire a private investigator to find out the location of Amanda Clark." Shelby began to gaze at the menu.

"Do you really want to find her, Shelby? If she doesn't know Robert is her father or that he is dead, we have nothing to worry about. Didn't you and Jerry already try to find her?"

"Preston, I believe you have a valid point." Shelby smiled and patted his hand. "Maybe you should stay sober more often, but we need to make sure she doesn't appear anytime soon; news of his death was all over the news; I'm surprised she hasn't shown up already."

Preston signaled the waiter. "Now that this discussion is over, I need to order something stronger than ice tea."

****

Delilah, Norma, and Jordan sat at a booth in Smash Burger. While waiting for their order, Jordan leaned back in his seat, "What happened at the reading of the will today?"

Delilah gave him a summary of the events in the lawyer's office. "Do you have any information about this Amada Clark?" Jordan asked. "Why wasn't she present at the reading of the will?"

Delilah shook her head. "I was told after the accident that CC only learned about the girl shortly before the accident."

Norma added, "Jerry and Shelby went to Gaylord, TX, Robert's home town several weeks ago, I assume they were looking for the girl; apparently, they never found her."

Delilah shrugged. "Your guess is as good as mine. Based on the conditions in CC's will, I bet Shelby and Preston hope she never shows up."

"Wonder what Jerry's up to," Jordan said taking a bite of his burger.

Norma laughed. "He's trying to figure out a way to get both Delilah and my share of the station."

Delilah held up a French fry. "My guess is Jerry is probably cooking the books now that Norma and I can demand to see how KLS is really being run."

"Why don't we just enjoy lunch and forget about the drama at the lawyer's office," Norma said smiling at Jordan.

"The next time we invite you to lunch the new partners at KLS will need to find a more upscale place to eat."

Delilah sighed, "Unfortunately we still don't know what really happened to CC."

"Just be patient," Jordan said, reaching across the table squeezing Delilah's hand. "The investigation is still active. Why don't the two of you focus on KLS and let me do the detective work."

Jordan rose and moved away dropping some bills on the table. "I'll be in touch," he said over his shoulder.

Delilah stood. "Let's get out of here and hit the mall. I need some retail therapy."

"Right behind you, Sherlock," Norma said grabbing her purse. *Delilah never shopped. Did this new interest in shopping have anything to do with Jordan?*

Chapter Thirty-Five

The door to Delilah's office opened with a bang. Shelby Clarke walked unannounced into her office. Norma came in behind Shelby and shut the door. "I'm sorry, Delilah, but MISS THING walked right pass me," Norma said with a shrug of her shoulders.

"Oh, look at you two co-conspirators trying to keep afloat what my mother spent most of her life building. This station was her life. 50 percent of that life was given away and if you think I'm going to let you get away with that; well think again." Shelby glared furiously at them.

"We didn't expect anything, Shelby; those were CC's wishes," Delilah said angrily.

"I don't believe you," Shelby spat. "Listen closely, I'm here to take back what you stole from my mother."

"How do you intend to do that?" Norma asked, putting her hand on her hip.

Shelby whirled around and faced Norma. "I have money now. I'll sue you both for every penny you have. I'll keep you in court so long you'll beg me to take this station off your hands."

Delilah jumped to her feet.

"While you are suing us maybe the judge would like to hear how; you kept your own mother a prisoner in her own house tied to a bed in her own filth."

"How do you know all this?" Shelby screamed. "Was it before or after you broke into our house?"

Delilah sat back down in her chair.

Shelby smiled. "Oh, I see I hit a nerve. Were you the one who pushed my mother into our pool? Maybe your boyfriend Jordan might need to look into that."

Shelby got up and walked to the door then whirled around and faced them. "See you in court."

Norma stared Shelby down. "Sue away Shelby. Nothing would make me happier than presenting your life, past and present, to the whole world; believe me, sweetie, I know plenty."

Shelby opened the door and stepped into the hall. "You have 30 days to turn over your portion of the station to me, or I'll see you in court." She slammed the door behind her.

"What now?" Norma asked slowly shaking her head. "Do you think she's bluffing? I can't believe Shelby would risk taking us to court; even she knows there are a lot of buried secrets that could be revealed."

Delilah turned to her computer and started typing. "If it's the last thing I do, I am going to find Amanda Clark and make sure she gets her share of Robert's fortune. The key to the whereabouts of Amanda Clarke seems to lead back to Gaylord, Texas."

Norma flopped down in the chair in front of Delilah's desk. "Let's get started."

Chapter Thirty-Six

Delilah turned off the interstate and drove several miles down the bumpy cracked road before Norma woke up from her nap and started reading the map. "Says here," she pointed at the map, "Gaylord is four miles down this road."

Delilah looked over at Norma and smiled. "We just drove through the city of Gaylord."

Norma rolled down the window. "You mean that ghost town back there is Gaylord, Texas?"

Norma pulled out her notes and handed them to Norma. "According to my Goggle search Gaylord, Texas was once one of the epicenters for oil production in Texas; second only to Spindletop. What happened?"

"Looks like the oil dried up and people moved away. Norma said looking out the car window. Everything is closed down; schools, post office, cafes, everything. Remember that movie Return to Bountiful where the lady went back to the town she grew up in and it was gone."

"Yes," Delilah said as she drove past a boarded-up movie theatre. "Remember the movie *The Last Picture Show*?"

"Let's get out of here," Norma said as she put the map back in the glove compartment. "This place gives me the creeps; besides there's no one here."

Delilah made a U-turn on the road and started back to the deserted town. "Not yet," Delilah said. "I saw an old man sitting on the porch of that general store in a rocking chair when we drove past. Maybe he knows if Amos Barlow is still alive."

Norma shivered. "If you saw anyone in this town sitting anywhere, it was probably a ghost. Let's go."

"Let's give it one more try," Delilah said as she turned off the engine and got out of the car in front of what appeared to be a store.

Norma got out of the car behind Delilah singing, "We've come this far by faith alone."

They both walked up the steps to the rickety porch that ran the length of the store. The empty rocking chair on the porch rocked back and forth in the stiff hot breeze.

"See I told you it was a ghost," Norma said as Delilah opened the screen door and walked inside the store.

The inside of the store was a step back in time. All cans and bottles were neatly lined up on shelves. Jams and jelly jars were lined up on the counter; some of the jars showing rust on the lids. An old cash register that might now be a valuable antique occupied the center of the long counter sitting beside a jar of gumballs that looked as if they were stuck inside the jar.

"Let's get out of here," Norma said grabbing Delilah's arm.

They both jumped as they heard a voice from the back of the store.

"Can I help you, ladies?" A short, gray-haired man dressed in dirty coveralls and a wrinkled, plaid shirt appeared from a room in the back of the store. He spat into a can as he walked behind the counter and set the can in front of him.

Delilah stated nervously, "Can you help us? We're writing a book about the old oil barons of Texas and we wanted to include Amos Barlow in the book. Doesn't he live around here?"

"Oil Baron." The old man threw back his head and laughed. "Look around you ladies see what's left of the Oil Baron's empire. He's responsible for what happened to this town." His eyes were misty as he looked out the window at the empty street.

"You should have seen Gaylord in its hay day." he said sadly. "A Saturday night in Gaylord was like a night in the big city. People came from miles around and crowded the town like a big city. Money flowed then, but in a blink of an eye it was all gone: thanks to Amos Barlow, there are only three people left in Gaylord; Joe, who runs the garage, me, and Amos Barlow."

"Amos Barlow is still alive?" Delilah asked as she exchanged an excited look with Norma.

"If you call drinking night and day is being alive." He spat again into the can.

"He lives down the road in that broken-down trailer. The only time you see him is when he drives down the road to Liberty to get more booze."

"Thank you for the information," Delilah said turning toward the door.

"No problem," he said as he held the door open for Delilah and Norma. "You're much nicer than the man and woman who were here a few weeks ago. They were so mean and nasty I told them Amos was dead. As soon as they heard that news, they flew out of town like a bat out of hell."

"Thank you, Mr.…." Delilah hesitated.

"Andrew Barlow," he said. "Amos is my twin brother."

"If we need anything more for our book, we'll contact you."

"Better do it quick," he said stepping out on the porch. "Old Joe at the garage is thinking of closing up and moving to Dallas to live with his daughter; Amos will more and likely drink himself to death and me they'll probably find my bleached bones in the back of the store."

"Why do you stay?" Norma asked.

"I promised my wife before she died that I would stay to the bitter end; and I have. When the three of us are gone, Gaylord will be gone forever."

"Get out of here," he said with a wave of his hand, "but do me a favor when you drive back through town, wave at me if Amos is still alive."

Chapter Thirty-Seven

Delilah drove slowly down the cracked rutted road until they spotted what must have been Amos Barlow's trailer. Making a U-turn Delilah parked the car on the side of the road and they both got out. A man who looked as if he weighed over 300 lbs. was sitting in a lawn chair under the only tree in the yard.

There was a six-pack of beer and a bottle holding what looked like whiskey sitting on a rusty TV tray next to him. An old dog stood up as they approached then laid back down beside the man in the chair. As a reward for his efforts, the man scratched the dog's head.

"Amos Barlow?" Delilah said in a squeaky voice.

The man looked at her with bloodshot eyes and snarled, "Who wants to know?"

"I'm Delilah Morgan. I'm writing a book on Texas oil magnates and your name was mentioned. I'd like to interview you." The lie was the first thing to come to her mind.

"Old, broke, oil magnate," he snarled. "Welcome to my kingdom," he said waving his arm, "or what's left of it." He lifted the bottle on the tray to his mouth and took a long swig.

"Oil was my world, Gaylord was my kingdom. I owned everything for miles around. But with one stupid mistake, I lost everything."

"Would you be willing to tell me what happened?"

"I trusted a man who was married to my daughter and he robbed me blind. Stole every penny I had ever made, then disappeared." He slammed the bottle down on the table.

"To make up for the lost I pumped oil night and day until all the wells ran dry. When the wells ran dry, people started leaving Gaylord; soon everyone was gone."

Delilah and Norma listened quietly. They could feel Amos's pain in every word.

"Stores closed, schools closed, every business in town held on as long as they could then were forced to close. Gaylord became a ghost town with only three ghosts left." There is a bright side to this story, he popped a tab on a beer can and took a deep draw from it.

"Over the years, Bobby Joe Clarke paid me back every penny he stole from me; but it was too late. I knew I could never bring Gaylord back so I just let it go."

"What happened to your family?" Delilah asked softly.

"My wife left after I lost my money and our home; her leaving wasn't much of a loss, but when my daughter and granddaughter left it broke my heart; I loved those two more than life itself."

Delilah felt defeated. "You never heard from them again? You didn't try to find them?"

"All I felt was defeated and ashamed; I had failed them," Amos said sadly. "I got a wedding invitation from my granddaughter some years back, but nothing after that."

Norma's ears perked up. "Did you by any chance keep the invitation?"

He laughed as he took another swig from his beer can. "I kept the invitation pinned on my board inside along with an envelope for Amanda if anyone finds her. Figured when someone found my dried, bleached bones they would notify my next of kin." He laughed a dry hollow laugh.

"Mind if I take a look?" Norma said moving toward the trailer.

"Why? Never mind, help yourself, but watch out for the roaches." He threw back his head and laughed.

Norma was inside the trailer in what seemed like thirty seconds and came out of the trailer, visibly shaking her head. She nodded at Delilah and started toward the car.

Delilah stood up, "Thank you, Mr. Barlow, for telling us a little about your life and about Gaylord."

Amos looked up at her with what appeared to be tears in his eyes. "Do me a favor, don't mention my name in your book. I've had enough embarrassment and shame in my life to last a lifetime; let me rest in peace."

"I'll respect your wishes, Mr. Barlow," Delilah said as she and Norma walked out of the yard and got into the car.

"Let's get out of this town," Norma said. "I've never been so depressed in all my life."

As they drove thru Gaylord, Norma rolled down the window and waved at Andrew Barlow on the front porch then dabbed at her eyes. "It's hard when you see your dreams die; especially when they're killed by someone you thought you could trust."

Chapter Thirty-Eight

Two Days Later

Delilah heard a knock on her office door. When she looked up, Norma walked in and sat down in the chair in front of her desk.

"Since when do you knock on my door?" Delilah asked looking up from a stack of papers piled in front of her on the desk.

Norma smiled. "I don't knock when I have bad news; I only knock when things are going right, and today things are definitely falling into place."

"Make it quick, Jerry has me buried in paperwork."

"Jerry's just mad because we voted him down and hired Jennifer Holland to take over your job on the radio; then you hired Jonathan to bring a new younger vibe to the station." Norma gave Delilah a smile and a thumbs up.

"Ratings and increased advertising have changed his mind," Delilah said laughing.

"Money always brings a smile to his face but don't think he still isn't trying to get us out of the station; permanently; but what is your news?"

Norma laughed, "Stop worrying about Jerry. He's left for the day to get ready for some social event he's attending tonight."

"So what plan are you hatching?"

"Road trip to Richmond Texas," Norma said smiling.

"Why would we be going to Richmond Texas?"

"No reason really except that's where Amanda Clarke lives."

"How did you find her?"

"Remember when I went into Amos's trailer to look at Amanda's wedding invitation, well the name of her perspective husband was on the invitation, plus the location of the wedding."

"And…"

"And Goggle and I went on a search, found her husband and Amanda Clarke Davis."

"When you smile like you're smiling now, I know there is more to the story."

"Well…" Norma drawled. She reached into her pocket. "I also took the envelope Amos had for her. WE can give it to Amanda when we find her."

Delilah grabbed her purse and shouted, "Road trip."

Chapter Thirty-Nine

Driving from Houston to Richmond, Texas didn't take long. Finding Amanda's house on the outskirts of town was another story. The rambling ranch-style house sat on a hill and looked down on a long sprawling lawn. As the two women drove closer to the house, they saw a small lake behind the house. Two young boys played Frisbee on the front lawn with a dog who labored to keep up with them. As Delilah and Norma got out of the car, the woman stopped watering her flowers and turned to look at them.

Both Delilah and Norma gasped. There was no mistaking that this was Robert Clark's daughter. She had the same long straight nose, the strong jawline, and the bright blue eyes. What really stunned them was her smile. It was the bright warming smile that Robert Clark had for almost everyone. It was a smile that always made you feel welcome, but it could also disappear just as quickly. It usually disappeared when he was confronted with CC and his children.

Delilah walked forward and extended her hand. "Amanda Clark," she said nervously. "I'm Delilah Morgan, I…"

Amanda ignored her hand and said with a sneer, "I know who you are. You took over Cassandra Clark's radio show after her accident."

Amanda didn't wait for a response from Delilah. "My mother listened to Cassandra Clark faithfully until she left the show."

"Your mother is still alive?" Delilah said in astonishment. "Virginia Clark?"

"I sure am," a voice said as a woman came around the side of the house.

"Alive and kicking."

The Virginia Clark who stood before them had not aged gracefully. Her long hair which fell to her shoulders in disarray was snow white. Her face was all sharp angles with deep, dark freckles scattered across what once must have been flawless skin. Her thin cotton dress hung loosely on a figure that was almost skeletal. At the moment she stood shoulder to shoulder beside Amanda clenching and unclenching her hands.

"I guess you probably know that Robert Clark died in a car accident some months ago," Amanda said hesitantly.

"God rest his soul," Virginia Clark said.

Good riddance, Amanda mouthed silently.

Amanda turned to her mother. "How can you still care about a man who left you high and dry years ago? Still care about a man who never did anything for you or me over the years?"

When her mother didn't answer, Amanda ranted on. "That man didn't care about you or me. If he had, you won't have had to struggle all these years."

"Your father loved you, Amanda," her mother said sadly.

"If he had loved me so much, why didn't he use all his millions to find us; to make life better for you?" Amanda said angrily; She didn't know what to say or do when her mother started to cry.

"You see what you've done," Amanda shouted. "You've upset her; what do you want?"

Delilah couldn't speak so Norma stepped into the fray. "Cassandra Clark left a third of Robert's estate to you, Amanda; She thought that it was only right that you share the fortune Robert made."

"I don't want or need Robert Clark's money," Amanda shouted. "Keep it. He should have given the money to my grandfather; that's who he stole it from."

"He did give back the money to your grandfather," Delilah said. "Over the years, Robert paid your grandfather back every cent he stole from him."

Virginia Clark looked at Delilah in amazement. "How do you know that?"

"We went to Gaylord a few weeks ago and your father told Norma and me the whole story. Your father is very much alive." Virginia began to cry again.

"So, he's still alive," Amanda said with a sneer. "What do you want us to do?"

Norma was angry. "Your grandfather is old and alone. Every day grieving over the loss of his family and the dream he spent his lifetime building. Watching his life slip away, knowing that no matter what he did, nothing will ever bring it back." Norma took a deep calming breath.

Virginia began sobbing again.

"No matter how you feel about Robert Clark, your grandfather loved you and over the years he has silently mourned the loss of you and your mother," Norma said quietly.

Delilah dug out the envelope they had taken from Amos's trailer and put it in Virginia's hand. "I don't know what's in this envelope, but maybe it will bring you some closure."

Delilah turned and started to walk away, "Here's the business card of the lawyer who is handling CC's estate." When Delilah attempted to hand the card to Amanda, Amanda let the card drop to the ground. Delilah turned and walked away, pulling Norma along with her.

When they were both in the car, Norma turned to Delilah. "This revenge thing is sad. We found Amanda, told her about the money, now the siblings can fight it out; I'm through."

"Not through yet," Delilah said.

"What's left to do?" Norma asked in a puzzled voice.

"Find out who killed CC; then our work is done," Delilah said with a sigh.

Chapter Forty

Delilah jumped when the red phone on her desk rang. It frightened her as she realized it was CC's private line and no one ever called her on it. No one except…

"What do you want, Norma?" Delilah said into the phone, "I've got work coming out of my ears; I don't have time to play around."

Norma's whispered voice came over the line, "You'll never guess who's in the lobby waiting to see you?"

Before Delilah could answer, Norma continued on, "Amanda Clarke Davis."

Delilah hesitated, "Well, tell her I'm busy. I can't see her today."

"She came to apologize, Delilah, the least you can do is see her."

Delilah didn't answer. "I thought you were looking for closure; now's your chance," Norma said breathlessly.

"Alright send her in; I only hope she doesn't throw another tantrum."

Delilah attempted to straighten out the mess on her desk when Norma ushered Amanda into the office. To Delilah's surprise, Norma didn't stay; she immediately left the office closing the door behind her.

Amanda sat down in the chair in front of Delilah's desk and placed her handbag on the floor.

"I know; you're probably busy so I won't take long. I just wanted to apologize for the way I acted the last time we met. I took out all the anger I held all these years for my father on you; that wasn't fair."

"I accept your apology, Amanda. I know Robert would be proud of the strong woman you've grown up to be."

"Thank you, Delilah, but let me tell you the rest of my news. There's more. My mother and I went back to Gaylord to see my grandfather." Her voice became choked. "It was worse than we could have imagined. To think he had been living like that all these years; old and alone thinking no one cared about him. My mother and I were heartbroken and so ashamed."

Delilah leaned forward and handed Amanda a tissue to blot her tears.

"What are you going to do about him? He needs help."

Amanda smiled, "We brought both my father and uncle back home to live with us as a family. The man who ran the garage has a grandson who moved him to Dallas a week ago."

Delilah said softly getting to her feet, "So Gaylord is now officially gone?"

"It's gone," Amanda said, "Along with the memories and sorrow that surrounded the town."

"I went to see the lawyer whose name was on the business card you gave me."

"And…" Delilah said.

"I turned over all the money to my mother; she deserves every penny."

"But what about you?" Delilah asked.

"I no longer have to deal with the anger and resentment I sometimes displayed over my past. I'm surrounded by ALL my family. The look my mother carried for years as she struggled to make ends meet is gone; I am truly happy now that she will have the freedom and security she has worked for all her life."

Delilah extended her hand to Amanda, "I'm glad everything worked out for you and your family."

The door to the office opened. Norma walked in followed by Shelby Clarke. With a triumphant smile on her face, Norma announced, "Shelby I would like you to meet your half-sister, Amanda Clarke Davis."

The color drained from Shelby's face; her eyelids fluttered as she fainted and fell to the floor.

****

As the three women struggled to get Shelby on the small sofa in the corner of Delilah's office, Jerry Wainwright walked onto the office. When he saw Shelby, he shouted, "What's happened? What's the matter with Shelby?"

He pushed Norma aside. "What have you two done to Shelby? Shelby will sue us, take the station, our money, everything," he groaned.

"I'm calling 911." Jerry yelled. "We need to get her medical attention."

"At a time like this all you can think about is money; forget about the money," Delilah said as she fanned Shelby's face with her hand.

"Who is this woman?" Jerry demanded gesturing at Amanda.

"Let me introduce you," Norma said, "This is Amanda Clarke Davis; Shelby's half-sister."

"Jerry." Shelby groaned as she attempted to sit up.

Jerry ignored Shelby and extended his hand to Amanda. "Amanda, so nice to meet you; I'm Jerry Wainwright, owner of KLS Radio."

"Part owner," Norma muttered under her breath.

"Why don't we go to my office; I have some idea on how to make your fortune double."

"Jerry, for heaven's sake, Shelby needs medical attention," Delilah declared.

Jerry turned as he ushered Amanda out the door, "You created the situation, you take care of it."

Delilah and Norma stared in astonishment as Shelby unsteadily got to her feet, straightened her clothes, and unsteadily walked to the door. "I'll deal with you two later." She shouted. "Where's Jerry?"

Delilah and Norma stood in the middle of the room staring at each other as Shelby staggered out of the office. "What just happened?" Delilah asked.

"Don't know; Don't care," Norma answered. "I'm out of here."

"On your way to Snookie's for your margarita?" Delilah asked flopping down in her desk chair.

"No," Norma replied, "I'm on my way to Homer's Club; dirty work requires a Dirty Martini."

Chapter Forty-One

As Delilah opened her front door and stepped out on her front porch, her cellphone rang; it was Norma. "Good morning, sunshine," Norma said cheerfully, "what are you up to?"

No, Norma, Delilah thought, *what are you up to*?

"I'm just leaving the house for the station; seems like I never get away from the station even on weekends."

"Delilah, you're going to the station on a weekend? Don't you get enough of that place during the week?"

"Actually, Jerry has some advertisers who want to meet me and this is their last day in town so I'm meeting them at the station. As a part-owner, you should also attend the meeting."

"Jerry at the station on a weekend that's never happened before. As long as I've known him, he has never worked on a weekend," Norma said. "He's too cheap to take you and his visitors to brunch; what a cheapskate. Too bad you're not available; I was going to treat you to brunch at Brennan's."

"If we finish early, maybe we can have lunch somewhere later."

"Tell you what; I'm on my way out. I will meet you at the station later," Norma said cheerfully.

"I'll probably be late. Do me a favor and turn on the green button behind my desk."

"What's the green button for?" Delilah asked completely puzzled.

"As you well know, Jerry is too cheap and too secretive to hire a secretary, so I record all his meetings. He goes over the tape later to see if he missed anything. He keeps the tapes in his office in case someone tries to sue the station or he can find another way to wring an extra dime out of a client. The station has needed a secretary and a financial manager for years, but Jerry has refused; wants to keep everything under wraps. To keep Jerry honest we'll continue to record meetings. Remember CC's warning to always watch your back."

"Try not to be late, Norma; I may need back up."

A horn sounded in the background.

"That's my ride," Norma said. "See you at the station."

"Your ride?" Delilah said.

"I own 25% of a radio station; I now use Uber – no more fighting traffic for me."

****

Delilah entered the empty lobby of KLS Radio. It was dark and she switched on the lights which flooded the lobby. Following Norma's instructions, Delilah pushed the green button behind Norma's desk. She went over to Jerry's office, knocked and stuck her head inside.

Jerry was sitting behind his desk, his fingers were entwined, and resting on his desktop.

Not seeing anyone in the office, Delilah, blurted out, "I hope I'm not too late; you know Houston's traffic, even on a Sunday."

Jerry smiled. "No, Delilah, you're right on time. It will give us time to talk privately for a moment; have a seat."

Delilah dropped her bag next to a chair in front of his desk and sat down.

Delilah settled in her chair and looked at Jerry; his face was flushed. "Did you manage to get any money from Amanda?"

Jerry leaned back in his chair and scowled. "Would you believe she is handing over all that money to her mother to manage. She wants no part of Robert's money; what an idiot. They'll run through that money in no time. I was only trying to give her some sound financial guidance, but she wouldn't listen."

Delilah leaned forward and said, "Well, I'm done with that part of the Clarke drama; I'm moving on."

"Moving on to what?"

Delilah looked directly at Jerry and said quickly, "Finding who murdered CC; that parts not over."

Jerry leaned forward. "I've been a little concerned about you, Delilah, you seem to be a little overwrought between your interest in the station and your unending crusade to prove CC was murdered. From listening to you lately, I can see you are not focused; that's got to stop. I would suggest that you concentrate more on your management issues and give up this ridiculous crusade to vindicate CC by proving she was murdered."

Delilah leaned forward in her chair. "I can't stop now, Jerry, I am getting closer and closer to finding out who killed both CC and also the person who killed the woman they thought was Lillian."

"Then let's not make this a suggestion, let's make it an order. As I told you before, let it go, concentrate on helping me keep this station alive and stop this investigating nonsense."

"Jerry, don't you want to know who killed CC?"

"I don't need to guess, I know who killed her."

Delilah froze.

Jerry laughed. "Lillian Barrett came to Houston, to get revenge on Shelby and Preston. She blamed them for what happened to her after her husband's death. Even though she, and she alone, had masterminded the plot; she still blamed them for everything that happened."

Delilah chimed in, "When she discovered that their financial wellbeing depended on CC, she abandoned them and started on CC."

"Bravo, Delilah, you are absolutely right. The strange thing was that CC and Lillian became friends. CC didn't have any real friends, and Lillian played her like a cheap guitar. Lillian fawned over CC; made her feel like the great lady she had once been. For all the adoration and attention Lillian paid her; CC paid dearly. That radio scheme she worked up with Lillian calling in begging for help raised her ratings, which really suited me. It was all made up."

"You knew about it and didn't do anything?" Delilah questioned.

Jerry ignored her question. "After Robert died, and CC inherited all his money, Lillian took the kid gloves off and started demanding more money."

"Why did she want more money?" Delilah noticed that Jerry's face was again turning red, and he was extremely agitated.

"Why, why, why. I'll tell you why. In one of her drunken stupors, CC told her some things that she shouldn't have and Lillian threatened to use the information against her. CC told her things that should have remained a secret and could have ruined her children, CC, and ME.

"CC called me on the phone and told me about Lillian's demands. She begged me to talk to Lillian. Make a deal with her to keep quiet, leave town, whatever. In exchange for my help, she would give me a huge amount of money, which she later did, and I was able to save KLS from financial ruin."

"Financial ruin? I thought the station was doing well."

"That's none of your business," Jerry said sharply. "KLS will survive, it has and always will; I needed the cash infusion CC offered so I went to see Lillian."

"I pleaded with her to take the money CC offered and get out of town. She laughed in my face and upped the ante. She gave me a figure for a ridiculous amount of money that she would accept to get out of our lives. I knew then she would never let any of us go until she bled us dry. I hit her once and she continued to laugh; then I lost control and hit her over and over again."

"You killed a woman you thought was Lillian?" Delilah was stunned. She stood up and backed away from Jerry's desk.

"When CC found out Lillian was dead, she went to pieces. She started drinking heavily again and making all kinds of threats. We had already had her confined to the house and fired all the staff, but it was becoming harder and harder to keep her confined."

"Did you have anything to do with Elizabeth Jones and Dorothy Stephens's deaths?"

"You have turned into quite a detective, Delilah." Jerry gave a low hollow laugh that frightened Delilah more than she wanted to admit.

"They came to the house to pick up some of Dorothy's things before we could move CC from the room we had confined her in back to her real room and they saw her. Shelby told me they planned to come back the next day and pick up the rest of Dorothy's things and get CC out of the house. They planned to bring the police if necessary, but I fixed that."

"Funny how one glass of sweet tea mixed with drugs can make you feel sick and slowly put you to sleep. It was too easy to get rid of both of them." He was closely watching Delilah for her reaction.

"You killed them too, Jerry, two harmless women; you are a monster."

He grabbed her arm. "Oh, you haven't heard the best part yet. After she heard about their deaths, she went completely crazy, ranting and raving about what she was going to do to me; to Shelby and Preston, to the whole world. She was going to expose all of us. In order to get Shelby and Preston to help me, I finally had to tell them the truth. Robert Clarke was not their father, I was. If CC had followed through with her threat to find Robert's real daughter and turn over all of his fortunes to her, they would be left penniless; Robert was not their father." Jerry gave a cruel hard humorless laugh.

"They both immediately jumped on the bandwagon."

"Shelby and Preston are your children?" Delilah gasped. "And they let you do that to their mother?"

"Save your pity for someone who deserves it. Those two money-grubbers would do anything for a dime. They could care less about their reputations as long as they have money. I grew sick of both of them the moment they came into the world. I felt nothing for them then; I feel nothing for them now."

"I can't believe you killed all those people just to keep a secret. Who cares that they weren't Robert's children? Who cares that you and CC apparently had an affair and Shelby and Preston were the result?"

"It was always CC's idea to keep it a secret. She needed Robert's money to finance her fairy tale lifestyle; I needed CC's money to maintain the station; so everything went hand in hand."

"Jerry, who would have cared about you and CC having had an affair years ago?"

"You don't live in the same world as CC and I; we would have lost something we had worked for all these years; our reputations."

"You killed four people to save your reputation; that's crazy."

"Crazy to you; not to me. I thought I had all my bases covered until that night I saw you break into CC's house. I didn't know if CC had some coherent moment and told you the whole story or not; so you became my next target."

"ME?" Delilah screamed.

"Who do you think locked you in that storage locker? I thought no one would ever find you, but your boyfriend managed to rescue you. If only he hadn't been watching over you, I would have gotten rid of you sooner. I killed them all and now I'm going to kill you; better now than never." He reached in his desk drawer and pulled out a gun.

Delilah turned over the chair in front of him causing him to fall back, giving her time to get to the door and open it. She rushed out into the lobby and saw Norma standing behind the reception desk.

"Put the gun down, Jerry," Norma ordered, "I've already called 911, they're outside now." The front door opened and two police officers, followed by Jordan Marsh, rushed into the lobby.

"Put the gun down and put your hands in the air," the policemen ordered.

Jerry slowly complied and lowered the gun to his side. He laughed, "I've done nothing wrong officer, this woman attacked me, I was only defending myself."

Norma reached under the desk and flipped a button and Jerry's voice boomed into the lobby: *I killed them all and now I'm going to kill you.*

Jerry's face registered disbelief. He turned suddenly and ran toward his office.

Jordan caught up with him and knocked him to the ground, grabbing the gun.

****

One day later, Delilah stood behind the reception desk as Norma thumbed through the pages of the Houston Chronicle newspaper.

"Jerry would be so upset to see he didn't make front-page news," Delilah said sadly. They both silently read the newspaper article.

KLS RADIO STATION OWNER/OPERATOR, ARRESTED FOR MULTIPLE HOMICIDES.

Delilah said quietly, "What is going to happen to Jerry?"

Norma closed the newspaper and turned to look at Delilah. "What we should be asking ourselves is what is going to happen to us?"